EXPECTING
A BOLTON BABY

—

SARAH M. ANDERSON

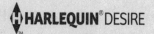

HARLEQUIN® DESIRE

Recycling programs
for this product may
not exist in your area.

ISBN-13: 978-0-373-73280-7

EXPECTING A BOLTON BABY

Bobby's Pulse Went From Pounding To A Dead Standstill In The Space Between Heartbeats.

Only one woman in the world looked like that.

Stella Caine.

Bobby rubbed his eyes, but the vision stayed the same.

Stella.

How was this possible?

Enchanting was all he could think as her hips swayed toward him. A long black fur coat almost swallowed her whole, except for the flash of leg that cut through the night with every other step. When she hit the circle of light that spilled out of his trailer, she looked up at him.

Her eyes, the palest of green, flashed at him. For all her edgy style, her eyes were something completely different—soft. Vulnerable, even.

"Hello, Bobby."

He wanted to pull her into his arms and tell her he wasn't going to let her out of his sight again.

But a gust of wind blew between them like a warning, and Bobby sensed just then that life as he'd known it was about to change.

* * *

Expecting a Bolton Baby
is part of The Bolton Brothers trilogy:

They live fast, ride hard and love fiercely!

Available only from Sarah M. Anderson
and Harlequin Desire.

* * *

If you're on Twitter,
tell us what you think of Harlequin Desire!
#harlequindesire

Dear Reader,

Welcome back to Crazy Horse Choppers, the family business run by the Bolton boys, three brothers: Billy (the creative one), Ben (the numbers guy) and Bobby (the salesman). They live fast, ride hard and love fiercely.

Bobby Bolton has the life he's always wanted—he's famous, thanks to the reality show he twisted his brothers' arms to get on television. He's wealthy—and he's going to be a whole lot wealthier by the time he gets done building his resort at the foot of the Black Hills. And when his resort takes off, he'll build a chain of upscale destination resorts that cater to lawyers and doctors who ride Crazy Horse Choppers on the weekend.

Yes, Bobby's got it all planned out—until the woman he can't forget, Stella Caine, walks back into his life and drops a bombshell he never saw coming—she's pregnant with his child. Suddenly, all of Bobby's plans are in danger of crumbling right before his very eyes. He'll have to decide what's most important—family or business?

Expecting a Bolton Baby is a sensual story about deciding what you really want. It's also my twist on cowboys and Indians—bikers and Indians! I hope you enjoy reading it as much as I enjoyed writing it! Be sure to stop by www.sarahmanderson.com and join me for the latest on The Bolton Brothers!

Sarah

SARAH M. ANDERSON

Award-winning author Sarah M. Anderson may live east of the Mississippi River, but her heart lies out West on the Great Plains. With a lifelong love of horses and two history teachers for parents, she had plenty of encouragement to learn everything she could about the tribes of the Great Plains.

When she started writing, it wasn't long before her characters found themselves out in South Dakota among the Lakota Sioux. She loves to put people from two different worlds into new situations and to see how their backgrounds and cultures take them someplace they never thought they'd go.

One of Sarah's books, *A Man of Privilege,* won the *RT Book Reviews* 2012 Reviewers' Choice Best Book Awards Series: Harlequin Desire.

When not helping out at her son's school or walking her rescue dogs, Sarah spends her days having conversations with imaginary cowboys and American Indians, all of which is surprisingly well-tolerated by her wonderful husband. Readers can find out more about Sarah's love of cowboys and Indians at www.sarahmanderson.com.

To Leah, the youngest by eight minutes.
Sometimes instant families really do work out!

One

What was Stella doing right now?

For the hundredth time this week, Bobby asked himself that question. And the answer was still the same.

He didn't know. But he wished he did.

Maybe he should have tried harder to get her number after that wild night at the club. Yeah, he should have. But Bobby Bolton didn't chase women. He enjoyed their company—usually for the evening, occasionally for a weekend—and that was that. He didn't do long-term, didn't do "relationships." Everyone had a good time and parted as friends. That was the way he'd always interacted with the opposite sex.

Until that night two months ago when he'd met Stella.

The last night he'd felt as if he had the world in the palm of his hand.

FreeFall, the TV network that had bought his reality show, *The Bolton Biker Boys,* had hosted a behind-the-velvet-rope party to celebrate the upcoming season. It was the sort of event Bobby lived for—glamorous people in a glamorous setting.

But even as he'd been doing some serious schmoozing, the woman sitting at the corner of the bar caught his eye. She'd had a sense of style that marked her as different—instead of too tight or too short, she'd had on a long-sleeved dress covered in leather straps and buckles that was completely backless. The outfit demanded attention, but the woman wearing it had been alone, her gaze trained on the crowd.

He hadn't known who she was when he'd bought her a drink. She'd told Bobby she was a fashion designer, but she hadn't mentioned her last name. She'd enchanted him with her outrageous sense of style, soft British accent and distance from the rest of the crowd. She'd been a woman apart—except for him. They'd talked as if they were the oldest of friends, every joke an inside one only they found funny. He'd been unable to resist her.

Which must have been how they'd wound up in the back of a limo with a bottle of champagne and a couple of condoms.

It was only afterward, when he'd asked for her number, that she'd dropped the bomb. She was actually Stella Caine, only daughter of David Caine—owner of FreeFall TV, distributor for Bobby's reality show, majority investor in Bobby's new resort and one of the most notoriously conservative men in the world.

He'd felt as if the rug had been pulled out from under his feet. How could he not have known who she was? How could he have done something so stupid? What would happen when she told her father?

David Caine would ruin him, that's what, and everything he'd worked for would be gone.

Even after revealing her identity, she hadn't given Bobby her number. Just a kiss on the cheek and an "It's better this way," leaving Bobby to wonder, *Better for who?*

And that had been the last he'd heard from her. He hadn't been called on the carpet by David Caine for corrupting his daughter. He hadn't received any calls or texts from Stella. He had nothing to remember her by, except a picture.

And the memories.

Just then one of the production assistants, Vicky, said, "We got the shot," shaking him out of his thoughts. "Anything else?"

Right. Bobby wasn't in New York. He was filming his show for FreeFall TV in South Dakota. And Stella Caine had made it clear that she didn't want anything from him beyond their one-night stand. He needed to stop thinking about her and focus on the job at hand.

And what a job it was.

"I think that's it for today," Bobby told Vicky as he looked around the narrow trailer that was his office and, most days, his home.

It was four on Friday afternoon in the middle of November, the setting sun already cloaking everything in winter gray. The construction workers had packed up for the day. Vicky and her film crew, Villainy Productions, had stayed later to get a couple shots of Bobby sitting at his desk, looking overwhelmed.

He had not done a lot of acting today.

What the hell was his problem? This was everything he'd ever wanted. His reality show had debuted on Free-Fall with impressive numbers. The production contract he'd signed with FreeFall had underwritten half the financing he needed to begin building Crazy Horse Resort, which was being filmed for the show.

Ten miles outside of Sturgis, South Dakota, the Crazy Horse Resort was going to be *the* upscale destination for weekend bikers—the doctors, stockbrokers and lawyers who made money hand over fist during the week and liked to cut loose in motorcycle leathers on the weekend. It'd be a five-star destination resort, complete with spa, shopping, three restaurants, a nightclub and a Crazy Horse boutique and garage so guests could upgrade their ride or buy a new one. It was the perfect synergy of business form and function and would turn Crazy Horse into a total lifestyle brand.

The reality show, featuring not only the construction of the resort but his family and their business, was also feeding a huge sales boom for his brother Billy's custom-made choppers. Crazy Horse Choppers was now an international brand with a loyal following among both celebrities and hard-core bikers, and Bobby was still the marketing director.

He had worked for years to get to this point. He was rich, famous and powerful. All of his dreams had come true. By all objective standards, he was a success.

So why the hell did he feel so...unsure?

Hours after everyone else had gone home, he sat at his desk, which was wedged against one wall of the construction trailer. The sales numbers for Crazy Horse were up on his computer screen, but he wasn't looking at them. *Maybe I'm just tired,* he thought, trying to get his eyes to focus. He couldn't remember the last time he'd been home.

Instead of sleeping on his California king bed with Egyptian cotton sheets, he'd been spending nights on the trailer's couch. Instead of cooking in his condo's gourmet kitchen, the one with marble countertops, he'd been using a hot plate, coffeepot and microwave. And instead of enjoying his Whirlpool-jet tub, he'd been making do with the trailer's closet-size bathroom. His days had become a blur of coffee, construction, cameras. Hell, he hadn't even made a business trip since he'd been to New York—two months ago.

Suck it up.

As his older brothers, Ben and Billy, constantly reminded him, he'd brought this on himself. They weren't about to step in and offer a helping hand. His brothers thought his ideas were ridiculous and expected him to fail, so Bobby would do whatever it took to prove them wrong.

Including living in a construction trailer and reviewing sales figures on a perfectly good Friday night.

Soon he would have his penthouse apartment on the top floor of the resort. He'd have a private elevator, expansive views of the Black Hills and—most important— he wouldn't be living in anyone's shadow. Not his father, Bruce, and his hopelessly out-of-touch way of running things. Not Billy and his insistence on building the bikes he wanted, not the bikes customers wanted. And not Ben and his slavish devotion to the bottom line.

He knew his brothers thought he was a screwup, but he'd show them. Nobody was going to mess up this deal.

For the first time in his life, Bobby would have something that was his and his alone. His own personal kingdom. He'd have complete control—hiring the chefs he liked, the designers he wanted. It was a big dream, but dreaming big was what he did best.

A car door slamming shut snapped him back to the present.

They'd had a few problems with copper thieves. Copper wasn't cheap and its resale value had recently gone through the roof. He had hired a security guard, but it took Larry about twenty minutes to drive around the entire site.

Then he heard it. Whistling. A jaunty tune, by the sound of it.

Not just thieves, but confident thieves. Bobby slid open the bottom drawer of his desk and grabbed his Glock. He'd gotten the gun a while back. He'd heard tales of contractors taking huge losses when their raw materials walked off. Insurance usually covered it—but then insurance rates went up. He refused to pay for the same materials twice.

They'd learn soon enough that no one stole from the Boltons.

He'd no sooner gotten the lock off the gun than someone knocked on the door. He jumped. Copper thieves didn't knock.

"Coming," Bobby said for lack of a better plan.

He shoved the gun into the back of his waistband. This could be Cass, the receptionist at Crazy Horse Choppers. She checked on him from time to time. Maybe she was stopping by to nag him about something.

Bobby opened the door. The light spilled out into the night, illuminating a…leprechaun? He blinked, but the image stayed the same. Short guy wearing a green vest over a plaid shirt underneath an overcoat, reddish hair sticking out from under one of those caps old men wore.

"Ah, there ye are," the leprechaun said in a distinctly Irish voice, giving Bobby a cocky grin. "Yer a tough feller to track down, laddie."

"Excuse me?" Bobby peered around the little man and saw a black sedan, the kind with windows tinted so dark they weren't legal in most states.

Suddenly, Bobby realized he'd seen that car—a Jaguar—around all week long, coasting past the construction site at odd times, the sleekness of the vehicle sticking out like a sore thumb.

He reached around his back, trying to be inconspicuous, trying to get a handle on the Glock.

The next thing he knew, he was looking down the barrel of a snub-nosed pistol. "Don't think that's the best idea, lad." The leprechaun held out his other hand. "Nice and slow."

"Who are you?" If Bobby was going to hand over his gun, the leprechaun owed him a name.

"The name's Mickey." Once he had Bobby's Glock in hand, he added, "That's a good lad. She said you were smart. I do hate to prove 'er wrong."

"What? She who?"

That got him another cocky grin. "Anyone else in here?" Mickey leaned in.

"No." Even though Bobby knew he should be keeping his eye on this Mickey, Bobby found himself staring at the black sedan, thinking *she?*

"Keep yer cool and we'll all be just fine." Mickey winked at him. "Sit tight and remember—" he brandished the pistol in Bobby's face again "—try anything funny and I'll 'ave to break my promise to 'er."

"What promise was that?"

"Not to hurt ye—at least, until she said so."

At this cryptic statement, Mickey pocketed both guns and turned back to the sedan. Still whistling, he opened the back door and held out a hand to the passenger.

A long feminine leg exited the vehicle, followed by a second equally impressive leg. Bobby's pulse began to pound. Maybe he wasn't about to be robbed. Maybe he was about to get lucky. Why else would legs like that be here at a time like this?

A gloved hand settled in Mickey's and a woman cloaked in black stood up. Even at a distance, Bobby could see the blunt black bangs and the severe bob that was three inches longer on one side than on the other. Bobby's pulse went from pounding to a dead standstill in the space between heartbeats.

Only one woman in the world looked like that.

Stella Caine.

Bobby rubbed his eyes, but the vision stayed the same. *Stella.*

How was this possible?

She stood for a moment, her eyes taking in the construction site. Mickey offered her his elbow, and arm in arm, they walked up to the trailer.

Enchanting was all he could think as her hips swayed toward him. A long black fur coat almost swallowed her whole, except for the flash of leg that cut through the night with every other step. When she hit the circle of light that spilled out of his trailer, she looked up at him.

Her eyes, the palest of green, flashed at him. For all her edgy style, her eyes were something completely different—soft. Vulnerable, even.

"Hello, Bobby."

A gust of wind blew between them like a warning. Bobby sensed immediately that, beyond the armed leprechaun, he was in danger. What had been cool and reserved in Stella the last time they'd met was nothing but arctic cold today. If she was happy to see him, she wasn't letting on.

"Stella." For a moment, he had no idea what else to say, which was something in and of itself. He always knew what to say, when to say it. It was his gift—the ability to read people and know *exactly* what they needed to hear. That gift had gotten him this far in life.

Apparently, it was going to fail him now. He didn't want to say anything. He wanted to pull her into his arms and tell her he wasn't going to let her out of his sight again.

But he knew that would probably get him shot. So the best he could come up with was, "Come in." He stepped to the side as she brushed past him, the scent of lavender surrounding him.

Mickey didn't follow her in. Instead, he leaned against the railing, oblivious to the winter temperature. "Keep yer cool," he told Bobby with a small salute. "I'd hate to 'ave to bust in, all un-gentleman-like."

What, did he think Bobby would do something to Stella? They'd already…well, they'd already spent time in each other's company. He wasn't the kind of man who'd hurt a woman. Bolton men took care of women.

For him, that usually meant that he made sure a woman was just as satisfied with their encounter as he was. He took care of her sexual needs, and she took care of his. Everyone went home happy.

But this? This wasn't the same thing. Not even close.

With a final confused look at Mickey, Bobby shut the door and turned his attention back to the woman looking around his construction trailer with obvious disdain. Again, he knew he should say the right thing—New York was a hell of a long way from Sturgis, South Dakota, no matter how one went about it. But again, his mouth failed him.

"Can I…take your coat?"

Stella turned her back to him, but he saw her loosening the belt on her coat. He stepped forward and placed his hands on her shoulders.

The fur slipped off her and into his hands, revealing

a sheer maroon lace that covered her arms and back but left nothing to the imagination. He stared at it for a moment before the pattern clicked into place—skulls. The lace formed tiny skulls. It was entirely ladylike and entirely out there—very Stella.

Below that, she'd sewn a leather corset. This continued down into a floor-length knit skirt that, from the back, seemed puritanical. Then she stepped free of him and he saw that the front of the skirt was divided by two long slits that went all the way up to her thighs.

Bobby's pulse began to pound again. Only Stella Caine could pull off something that left her completely covered while still revealing so damn much. What was she doing here? And why did he still want her so badly?

He was taken with the sudden urge to kiss the back of her neck, right under the precise line of her hair. If he recalled correctly, he'd done the same thing once before, pinning her against a back door as they made their way out to the car.

He fought against that urge something fierce. The odds that Mickey would consider that "something funny" were too great. So Bobby hung her coat on the hook on the back of the door. "Would you like to have a seat?"

Her gaze cut a swath through the room before it landed on the couch at the other end of the trailer. He saw it now through her eyes. It was lumpy from where he'd slept on it and someone had spilled coffee on it at some point.

"Thanks, no," she said in a crisp tone, her hands smoothing down her skirt.

Scrubbing a hand through his hair, Bobby glanced down at her feet. Black suede boots with more buckles, the heels had to be four inches if they were one. He had no idea how far she'd traveled today, but he couldn't imagine that standing in those shoes were comfortable.

"Here. Let me get this for you." His desk chair, at least, was relatively new leather.

He wheeled it over to her. With a nod of appreciation, she settled in—and crossed her legs. The slits of the dress did not contain her right leg. The boot went almost up to her knee, but there was something about the flash of skin, from knee to upper thigh, that was unbelievably erotic.

For lack of anything better to do, Bobby took up residence on the lumpy couch.

He *needed* to say something.

But as he sat across a cluttered construction trailer from the most enchanting woman he'd ever met, he had nothing. He didn't know why she was here or what she wanted, which meant that he didn't know what she needed to hear. All he knew was that his Glock was outside with an Irishman who probably wouldn't hesitate to shoot Bobby with his own gun.

That, and he'd never been so glad to see a woman in his life. Which didn't make sense, because she sure as hell didn't seem all that glad to see him.

Finally, he couldn't take the silence anymore. "Your dress is stunning."

Her smile was stiff. "Thank you. I made it, of course."

"Where did you find skull lace?"

When her eyes narrowed, he realized he'd said the wrong thing.

"I made it," she repeated, her accent clipping the words.

"You *made* the lace?"

"It's called tatting, if you must know. It's my own design, my *own* creation."

He stared at the fabric. From this distance, maybe ten feet, he couldn't see the skulls. It fit her like a second skin. "Amazing." He meant the lace, but he realized he was looking her in the eyes when he said it.

A pale blush graced her cheeks. "Thank you," she said again, her voice softer. Then she dropped her gaze.

That, at least, had been the right thing to say. But he

knew she hadn't come all this way to fish for compliments. So he tried again.

"Mickey seems like an…interesting fellow. Have you known him long?"

"Since—a very long time."

Okay, so they weren't going to talk about Mickey. Which left him out of ideas. If she wasn't going to give him anything to go on, what could he do?

Luckily, Stella saved him from himself. "This is lovely," she said, looking around the trailer again. She managed to sound ironic and humorous and cutting.

"Isn't it?" he said, relieved to have a conversational opening. "Nothing but the best. I have a condo downtown," he felt compelled to add. "But that's just until the resort is finished. I'm going to live on-site when it's done."

Man, this was not going well. That came out as if he was trying too hard. Which he was. Confusion did that to a man.

Where was the smooth? Where was the ability to talk to anybody, anytime, anywhere? Where was the man who hadn't been able to keep his hands off this very woman?

He didn't like feeling this off balance. It was unfamiliar and unsettling.

"You haven't been to your flat in a week."

Bobby gaped at her. What did she want? Obviously, she hadn't come all this way just to stalk him into making awkward small talk.

"I've been working on the resort. Would you like to see the blueprints?" He sounded lame, even to his own ears, but he was desperate to establish some sort of connection with her.

She didn't answer. Instead, she stared him down.

God, he wished he could make sense of that look—angry and frustrated, as if she was barely clinging to her better manners. But underneath all of that, he sensed something else churning in her delicate eyes.

She was worried.

Finally, she moved. She wiped a black fingernail down the side of her lip, as if she'd eaten something she found distasteful. Then she took a deep breath, squared her shoulders and launched a verbal grenade into the middle of the room.

"I'm pregnant."

Two

Her words blew Bobby to shreds. Had she just said—*pregnant?*

She was staring at him, her face nearly blank as she waited for a response. What the hell was he supposed to say? His mouth opened, ready to ask who the father was, but the part of him that was good at talking knew that was the exact wrong thing to say.

Underneath her careful blankness, he could see she wasn't just worried—she was scared. Scared of what he was going to say, what he was going to do. But she seemed determined not to let him see that.

Well, that made two of them.

Then he realized. Whatever the truth was—and he was sure as hell going to get to that—she believed he was the father. That was, hands down, the most terrifying thought he'd ever had.

No one had ever said, "Bobby, you'll make a great dad someday." Instead, they usually told him to grow up. His brothers said those exact words all the time.

Kids were…messy. Loud. Unreasonable. Prone to screaming for no good reason. *Demanding.*

Bobby liked things his way. He liked staying out late, sleeping in later. He liked not having to rush home. He liked not having to step over toys or change diapers. Maybe all that stuff suited his brothers, but not him.

He wasn't father material. He was a businessman and

a damn good one. He was focused on making his resort the biggest draw in all of South Dakota. Hell, in either Dakota. And if things went as planned, there could be a chain of Crazy Horse Resorts across the West. A family wasn't in his plans.

Until now. Maybe.

He chose his words carefully. "I thought...we used protection. Both times."

At first, Stella didn't appear to move, but then he noticed that her chest rose and fell with bigger and bigger gulps of air. Finally she said, "We did."

Then how did she know he was the father? That was the question Bobby was dying to ask, but it probably wouldn't *ever* be the right thing to ask.

"I believe," she went on, her words precise and careful, "that the second condom failed. And that we were too sloshed to appreciate that fact."

"Oh." He tried to think. He'd had a couple of drinks in the bar, then they'd gotten a bottle of champagne to go. He didn't remember being drunk. He just remembered the way she'd unleashed an amazing amount of sexual energy on him. No amount of alcohol could touch that memory.

He ran his hands through his hair. He was coming apart at the seams, but she sat there, as calm as if she'd just announced that she'd like a nice pinot noir with dinner. He was so glad she was here—he'd done nothing but think of her for months. But...pregnant? Looking at him with such disdain?

He wanted to see her, but with that wry smile on her face. He wanted to make her laugh, to feel her body under his hands.

Bobby made a snap decision. He still wasn't sure exactly what she wanted from him, but he knew one thing. She didn't belong here, not where camera crews and construction workers came and went. She needed someplace private, someplace more fitting to this situation.

He stood so quickly that she startled. "We should go."

"Go?"

"Back to my place. We can get this—" he managed not to say "mess" "—we can get things sorted out there. You'll be much more comfortable—it's nicer, more private."

"No cameras?"

It was the first time he heard a note of undisguised worry in her voice. It only made him want to protect her. "No," he quickly agreed. "No cameras."

Cameras would only make his worst fear come true sooner rather than later. The reason he hadn't tracked down Stella, despite being unable to think of any other woman for two whole months? Because he was in no mood to find out exactly how quickly David Caine could ruin his life.

Hell, if Caine even knew his daughter was here, much less that she was pregnant—it would be all over. The show, the money to build the resort. He couldn't risk losing everything he'd worked for.

He moved to the door but made sure to open it slowly. "Mickey? Can you come in here?"

Although the little man had been standing out in the cold for close to twenty minutes, he didn't show it. True, he had his hands in his pockets, but Bobby got the feeling that was more to keep a grip on the guns than to warm his extremities.

Mickey nodded and stepped into the trailer. "Everything all right?" he asked Stella, who was now standing, her hands clasped in front of her.

"Yes."

"I wanted to confirm with you that it'd be best to move this conversation to a more private location—my condo. That way, Stella will be in an environment she'll find more comfortable."

Mickey looked confused. "He always talk like that?" he asked Stella.

"Not always," she murmured, dropping her gaze again.

Bobby hadn't meant to talk as if he was closing a deal with Mickey. It had just happened. Second nature.

Mickey looked to Stella, who nodded.

"You can follow me," Bobby said, getting Stella's coat.

"No worries, laddie." Mickey's impish grin was back. "I know where ye live." He turned back to Stella.

"I'll ride with Bobby."

If this announcement surprised Mickey, he didn't show it. Instead, he nodded. "See you there." Still whistling, he headed out toward his vehicle. With Bobby's gun still in his pocket.

Bobby knew what that meant.

He still had to keep his cool.

Bobby had a very nice car, a fire-engine-red Corvette. It fit with Stella's mental image of him as a consummate player. He'd certainly been one the night they'd met, his blond hair slicked back, the custom-fit gray suit over a white shirt—no tie, though. He'd looked as if he'd belonged at that party—as if he would have belonged at any party—whereas she'd been deeply uncomfortable even just sitting off to the side.

She couldn't reconcile his reaction to her announcement, though.

She wasn't sure what she'd expected him to do when she told him he'd fathered the baby growing in her belly.

No, that wasn't true. If she was being honest with herself, she'd expected him to tick down the reasons why he couldn't possibly be the father, why it had to be someone else. Or maybe she'd thought he'd flat out say that, even if it was his—which it wasn't—he would have nothing to do with it. With her.

But he hadn't. He'd just asked a few clarifying questions. Then suggested he drive her home.

Which he was doing now. They sat in the car in silence.

Stella wanted him to say something. The only problem was, she didn't know what she wanted to hear.

"Have you been here all week?"

His sudden question made her jump. Of course, at this point, she was already jumpy. Something about being unwed and pregnant had her on edge.

"Ah, no. I arrived on Wednesday." She wanted to look at him again, but sitting in the car made that awkward. Besides, looking at him did some…odd things to her. She pushed aside the fluttery emotions that had her glad to see him. She wasn't here for him. She was here for the baby. "Mickey drove out last week. He decided that Friday night would be the best time to catch you. I didn't think so, but he insisted."

"Thought I'd be out on the town?"

That's exactly what she'd thought, but she didn't want to admit it. Instead, she redirected. "I learned a long time ago to trust Mickey's instincts."

"Does your father know where you are?"

Even though they were in a dark car and Bobby wasn't looking at her, she kept her face blank. Years of training were impossible to override. It always came back to David Caine, sooner or later.

What would her father do when he found out about her condition? Would he insist she get married and hope no one counted the months? Would he publicly disown her and cut her off? Her fashion design business had a few loyal clients, but she couldn't cover the rent on her flat in SoHo by herself. Even though her father hadn't been there for her, he did pay the bills for both her and Mickey. Most of the time, it was the only connection between them. She didn't want to know how far her father would go to protect his "good" name.

"No. I'd prefer to keep it that way."

"Understood."

She heard him exhale, saw his hand clench the steering wheel far too tightly as the car turned through a grand apartment complex. No doubt he had a laundry list of reasons to keep this from her father, too. Bobby pressed a button and a subterranean garage door opened. Then they pulled underneath the building.

After he put the car in Park, he got out and came around the side to open her door. He even held out his hand for her. She didn't know if he did it because he'd seen Mickey do it or if this was how he treated all the women he brought back to his place. That thought sent a spike of pain through her, though, so she pushed it aside as she stood.

He didn't let go of her hand. They stood there, her hand in his, less than a foot of space between them. Heat flared—the same heat that had gotten her into this fine mess. Why had she let something as ridiculous as desire ruin everything? She should pull away, break this connection between them. She should have pulled away two months ago, too.

Despite her heeled boots, he was still tall enough she had to look up at him. His sandy-blond hair was tousled, week-old scruff on his jaw, his eyes a tad bloodshot. Not quite the player from her memory, but his mussed state didn't detract from his handsomeness. Instead, it made him more real.

And he hadn't yet told her this was her problem to deal with.

Stella's throat caught with unexpected emotion. For some ridiculous reason, she wanted to thank him for not rejecting her outright. Ludicrous hormones, she thought, shaking off the feeling. Just because he hadn't kicked her to the curb yet didn't mean he still wouldn't. He was just in shock, that was all.

And the fact that she felt that same pull—the one that had started all the trouble to begin with…? How she'd been drawn to his wide smile? How, even though she knew she had no business flirting with a man in a club, she'd been unable to resist him—his laugh, his touches? She'd tried to tell herself that she just needed a little fun and he fit the bill, but she wasn't sure that was true anymore—if it had ever been. She'd had no intention of picking up a man that night. But he'd changed everything from the very moment his smile had sent flashes of heat across her body.

That was all irrelevant now. She was not here for him, no matter how handsome he looked or how stunningly good he had made her feel two months ago. She was here for the baby.

Then he said something that took everything she thought she understood about the situation and turned it upside down.

"It's really great to see you again."

She froze, afraid to move, afraid to break the spell of the moment. Why on earth would he say that? It couldn't be because he was actually thrilled by her pronouncement. No, there was too much fear in his eyes for that, despite the admirable job he was doing of hiding it.

What if that was what he thought he had to say? What if the fear wasn't so much because she was expecting, but because of who she was—David Caine's daughter? What if he was being a gentleman about this because he was afraid of what her father would do when he found out?

She couldn't keep this quiet forever. Even if she managed to avoid her father for the duration of her pregnancy—which would probably be easy enough—sooner or later someone would notice that she was packing around an infant to photo shoots. Sooner or later, Mickey would break.

The time would come when she'd have to deal with her father. She wanted—needed—to deal with Bobby first. If she didn't have everything arranged... Bobby's promise to keep her secret was first. She'd like to get a promise of support from him, too, but she wasn't about to set up the baby for the heartbreak of being rejected by a father. She'd had enough of that for one lifetime.

In the middle of this thought, Bobby's other hand brushed under her chin and he kissed her cheek.

Stella heard herself say, "Even though…?"

It sounded pathetic and needy and everything she didn't want to be. Everything she wasn't, by God.

"Even though," he agreed, the scruff on his chin scratching her cheek. Then he seemed to realize that, despite the fact that he'd promised comfort and privacy, they were still standing in a minimally heated, semipublic car park. "Come on."

He tucked her hand under his arm, a perfectly chivalrous thing to do under the circumstances. But she felt the heat flow between them. She remembered how he'd acted in the club—suave, sophisticated. Fun. Sexy. Tonight he was…different. Even more appealing.

No.

She'd made that mistake once. She couldn't let her attraction to him cloud her thinking again.

He led her past a rather dramatic, electric-blue motorbike and to an elevator. "That yours?"

He nodded as they waited for the doors to open. "Built it myself. But I don't ride it when it's this cold. Probably won't take it out until April. It's been winterized."

The doors opened and they stepped in. The whole time, he kept his grip on her hand.

They rode to the top in silence.

Even though.

Even though she'd been foolish enough to get pregnant. Even though she'd been foolish enough to break one of her long-standing rules about clubs and parties and men and sex. Even though she was David Caine's daughter, for crying out loud, he was still glad to see her.

Sure, they'd had a lovely time at that party, an even lovelier time in her car afterward. In fact, it had been fun. Not just the sex—and that had been amazing—but the whole evening, from the very moment she'd seen him.

The music had been far too loud, of course, but that had given her a good reason not to talk to anyone. From her perch at the bar, she'd had an excellent view of the front door and was busy mentally preparing what she would say to her father when he came in. But Bobby had walked in instead, his blond hair and light gray suit standing out in the sea of New York black. She hadn't been able to take her eyes off him.

Which had been why he'd caught her staring. She remembered the first moment, the way his face had registered shock—no, surprise. *Excitement.* She couldn't remember the last time someone had been excited to see her.

Bobby had kept his eyes on her as he made the rounds of the club. He had been popular, that she could tell. He chatted with everyone—a handshake, a slap on the back, a joke, from the looks of all the laughing. But his gaze had always returned to her. And once he'd made his rounds, he'd made his way to her.

She'd braced herself for the come-on—for him to say, "So you're David Caine's daughter—I had no idea you were so beautiful," or something ridiculous like that. She'd heard them all and had long since learned not to take the so-called compliments personally.

But the line hadn't come. "I have a feeling there's more to that dress than the front," he'd said, leaning in close so he didn't have to shout over the music.

Her dress. The one she'd designed.

So she'd stood and done a small turn for him, feeling ridiculous. Until she'd gotten back around, facing him, and had seen something unexpected on his face.

Appreciation.

He'd been close enough to touch her then, but he hadn't. He'd waited until she'd given him the permission that came with her touching the seams of his suit—that came with her running her hands over his shoulders and down his back.

She shouldn't have touched him, shouldn't have allowed

him to touch her back. Small touches that had set her head spinning, clever observations that had made her laugh. A drink. His hand around her waist, leaning in close to whisper. His lips grazing her ear, then abandoning all pretense, his teeth scraping her lobe.

Her, saying, "Would you like to get out of here?"

She should have stopped it then.

But she hadn't wanted to. He'd been a stranger—only when she'd done a little digging over the next few days, wondering if the wonderful man from the club would look her up or not had she realized who he was. A reality-TV star. On her father's network. Which meant he'd signed a contract with her father's world-famous morals clauses.

So she'd stopped digging. Ignorance was bliss and she had no intention of harming him. She'd let that night live on in one perfect memory.

Then she'd missed her period.

Now, here she was again, knowing it was foolish to want him and wanting him all the same. He was glad to see her. And she wanted another moment of connection, of impulse. Of doing something she wanted for no other reason than she wanted to. She hadn't stopped wanting it. Not since she'd refused to give him her number, not since she'd missed her period and not since she'd gotten the positive test result.

But she didn't want to feel that pull again. Wanting Bobby would only muck up the works. She'd convinced herself the drinks had given that evening such a rosy glow. Faced with the decidedly nonlovely prospect of a squalling, shrieking baby, Bobby would do what any good player would do. He'd turn tail and run.

But he hadn't.

Maybe he'd wait until he knew which way the wind was blowing—until he knew what her father would do. He hadn't gotten to where he was by being a shoddy businessman, after all.

She wasn't here to destroy Bobby by bringing her father's wrath down on him. Why would she? For one night, in Bobby's arms, she'd felt free. Beautiful. Loved.

Perhaps she shouldn't have come. She should have gone straight to her father, claimed she had no idea who her baby's father was and insisted that she would raise the child on her own. Her father would have been unable to connect her and Bobby. She thought. But she couldn't be positive. As one of the richer men in England, David Caine had plenty of resources to backtrack her movements for months at a time.

And that, more than anything, was why she was here. If she was going to bring the dogs of her father's conservative-marriage war down on Bobby, she at least owed him a warning. Her baby was his, too.

Bobby ushered her down a long hallway and unlocked a door that looked just like all the other doorways they'd passed. He went in first and turned on the lights before closing the door after her.

"Here we are."

Stella took as deep a breath as she could in this bodice and stepped into Bobby's home. The place was quiet, with no signs that anyone had been here in a great while.

"Yes. Lovely."

The apartment wasn't what she'd expected, but that was starting to be a running theme when it came to Bobby. The lines were sharp, the colors—shades of gray and white, with splashes of vivid red abstract paintings for accent—were bold. The furnishings wouldn't be out of place in a New York loft—much like the one she lived in. None of those hideous overstuffed recliners that Americans seemed so fond of. Instead, a black leather seating group was tastefully arranged. The dining table was polished black glass, big enough to seat eight, with only a small picture frame set on one end. The whole place was spotless, nary a mote of dust to be seen. It looked as if he could host a cocktail party at a moment's notice.

This space was something he'd clearly put a great deal

of thought into. Suddenly, she wished she'd taken him up on his offer to look at the blueprints for his resort.

He moved to stand behind her, and she quickly undid the belt of her coat. Her fur skimmed down her shoulders, as sensual a feeling as she'd had in the past two months. She could feel Bobby's warm breath on the back of her neck. All she wanted to do was lean back into his arms and feel his body pressed against hers. Could he tell? Did he know the effect he had on her? He might. He'd kissed her there before, after she'd made the impulsive decision to have a little fun, for once.

It was an impulse she should have ignored.

The coat pulled free of her arms, leaving her shivering. Which she tried to convince herself was due to the sudden change in core body temperature—not the memory of Bobby kissing her. Then Bobby's hand was on the small of her back, guiding her toward the kitchen.

"Have you eaten?"

"Beg pardon?"

She saw the hint of a smile—warm and inviting—curve up the corners of his mouth. "I haven't had dinner. I'll make us something."

There it was again, that odd feeling that she couldn't quite name. Was he being his charming self or…was he taking care of her? It was the same feeling she'd gotten when he'd wheeled his desk chair out for her in that terrible trailer.

No one, aside from Mickey, had taken care of her since her mother died seventeen years ago. Stella had only been eight. By now, the memories of her mother were hazy around the edges, so much so that Stella was no longer sure what had happened and what she'd created. But she had fond memories—memories she clung to—of Claire Caine wrapping her in a fluffy towel after a nice bath, drying her off, helping her into her favorite pair of Hello

Kitty pajamas and tucking her into bed with a long story. Claire had done all the voices, too.

Stella had felt warm and safe and loved. Very much loved.

Then it had all gone away.

She blinked away the memories of the cold years that had followed Claire's death. Bobby was rummaging around in a rather large icebox. If he hadn't been home for a week, what on earth did he have in there that would be edible? Just thinking about it made her delicate stomach turn.

She backed out of the kitchen before any punishing scents could assault her nose. The morning sickness—a comical term if she'd ever heard one—had been manageable all day, unlike the day she'd flown out here. She'd spent all of Wednesday and most of Thursday in bed at the hotel, sipping ginger ale and nibbling dry toast.

"Beg pardon, but where's the loo?"

His arms full, Bobby's head popped up. "The what? Oh, yes. Sorry. Last door down the hall. Feel free to look around."

It's not as if she would snoop, really. He *had* given her permission to at least open a door or two.

So after she used the loo, she opened. One room had a pool table in it; another had a rather large telly and stadium seating. The third had a crisply made bed that was so large it had to be a California king.

Did he have someone sleeping in it with him? Perhaps he was the sort of fellow who brought home a different girl every night. It was entirely possible, after all. All she really knew about him was that he *was* the sort of fellow who left a club and had sex in a car.

When she walked back into the kitchen, the smell of food—eggs and cheese, bacon and veg—hit her. Suddenly, she was ravenous.

Bobby stood at a small island, whisking something. He had a dish towel draped over one shoulder, a chopping board and a knife in front of him. She could see a stove with several pans heating behind him. He seemed completely at ease doing all of this—not fumbling about, as she might have expected.

"Smells delicious."

His head popped up, a pleased smile on his face. "Veggie frittata and bacon."

"You…cook?" It wasn't the most diplomatic statement, but perhaps they were past the point of diplomacy. "No offense."

"None taken." His grin seemed heartfelt. "It doesn't mesh with my image, does it?"

"Not really."

"Promise me you won't tell my brothers, okay? They don't place a lot of value on cooking."

Ah, yes. The brothers. His show, *The Bolton Biker Boys,* was about the whole family. The press release she'd found said so. She didn't watch telly much and hadn't looked him up on YouTube—couldn't bear to watch her father's shows and know that he'd spent more time on them than he had with her. "Then how did you pick it up?"

"I spent more time with Mom," he replied, checking on a pan. He flipped something—peppers?—before continuing. "Billy's eight years older than me, Ben's five. They were always off doing their own thing while I was still in grade school. Mom would pick me up from school, then we'd head home and get dinner ready together."

Part of her chest started to hurt. The whole thing—a sweet mum to cook and talk with, to spend time with—that's what she didn't have. What she'd always wanted. "Do you still cook with her?"

His back still to her, he froze. "She died. When I was eighteen."

"I was eight. When my mum passed."

The words escaped her lips before she quite knew she was saying them. She didn't tell people about Claire. She'd long ago learned that talking about her mother was something not to be tolerated, as if speaking of her would sully her. Her father claimed it hurt too much. Maybe seeing Stella had made him hurt too much, too. Maybe that was why she rarely saw him at all. That had hurt almost as much as her mum's death—being ignored by her father, foisted off to boarding schools and Mickey.

She'd already pushed aside the hurt again—it was easy when one had as much practice as she had—but the next thing she knew, Bobby had set his bowl down, come around the island and wrapped her in a strong hug. The contact was so unexpected—so *much*—that Stella felt rooted to the spot. People didn't usually touch her. Even Mickey just offered her his arm. Her father hadn't touched her in years. Decades. She couldn't remember the last time she'd been touched like this.

No, she took that back. She could remember. Bobby was the last person who'd put his arms around her. The last person to hold her. As if she meant something to him.

"I'm sorry," he murmured into her hair, his hands pressed firmly against her back. "That must have been really hard on you."

Her throat closed up, pushing Stella toward tears. Where the bloody hell was all this emotion coming from?

Ah, yes. Hormones. She was pregnant, after all.

"Thank you," she managed to say without bawling.

After a small squeeze, Bobby leaned back. "You okay?"

"Fine, yes."

She managed to push the sorrow back down. What she needed to do here was focus not on the unchangeable past, but the very changeable future. She was pregnant. She'd do anything to make sure her child didn't suffer the same joyless fate she had.

Bobby let go of her and turned back to the stove. Heavens, the food smelled delicious. Part of her wanted to just enjoy this moment. He was making her dinner. He'd comforted her when she'd gotten upset. Wouldn't it be lovely if this were something she could look forward to on a regular basis? Wouldn't having someone to rely on—someone besides Mickey, that was—be just…wonderful?

It was a shame it wasn't going to happen, Stella thought as Bobby flipped slices of bacon. He was being delightful now because it was a wise business maneuver. In no way, shape or form was this an indicator of things to come, no matter how nice it was. She hadn't come for a husband. She'd come because it was the proper thing to do, to warn him. To give him a chance.

That's all she wanted for their baby. A chance.

Quickly, Bobby had plated up slices of omelet and bacon and added buttery toast browned in the oven. "I don't have any tea," he said apologetically as the coffeepot brewed.

"No worries. This smells amazing."

He carried the plates over to the table, setting them down next to each other. The table was empty, save for the picture frame she'd noticed when she'd first entered the flat, but he'd set the plates right next to each other, anyway. Close enough to touch, really. The proximity felt cozy.

Then she saw the picture in the frame.

Three

As Bobby set down the plates, the coffeemaker beeped. He hoped the coffee would be okay. His sister-in-law, Josey, hadn't been able to touch the stuff when she'd been pregnant. The smell had bothered her.

It wasn't until he was carrying the cups to the table that he realized what Stella was doing.

Holding the photo. *Studying* the photo.

"This is…*us*," she said in a voice so soft it was almost a whisper.

Immediately, Bobby knew why Stella was here. It wasn't just that she was pregnant, although that was a huge part of it. That one word was why she was here. To see if there were an *us*.

Damn.

If this were a normal negotiation, Bobby would do whatever it took to give Stella what she wanted. But…*us?*

She hadn't wanted an *us*. She'd made that blisteringly clear with her "don't call me, I won't call you" attitude. And once he knew who she was, he couldn't really blame her. If David Caine were his father, he'd do everything in his power to avoid irritating the man. Bobby had abided by her wishes. He'd not taken her out to lunch the next day, not tracked her down in the past two months.

He should have. If he'd had any idea she was pregnant, he would have. He fought the urge to drop everything and pull her into his arms. Again. The pull to protect her was overwhelming. But then, the pull to track her down had been, too.

This—the pregnancy, his need for her—was a problem.

He did not have time to drop everything and start playing house with anyone, let alone Stella Caine. Maybe in a few years, sure. The resort would be turning a profit, he'd have his penthouse apartment…then he might like to have someone in his bed who set his blood racing and made him laugh. But now?

So he did the next best thing. He told her only part of the truth.

"I get snapshots of all the celebrities I meet. I have a whole wall of them at the shop." All true. Nothing wrong with anything he'd just said. "It's good for our brand image—creates desirability." When she didn't say anything, he felt compelled to keep talking. "It's a good shot."

It was. Bobby had his arm around Stella's waist, but she had her back turned to the camera, revealing that swath of creamy skin left bare by the backless dress. She looked at the camera over her shoulder, a wicked pixie grin on her face. Her eyes bright, her hands rested on Bobby's chest.

What the camera didn't show was that, seconds before the paparazzi had snapped the photo, Bobby had been kissing her in that delicate spot right beneath her ear. The photo also didn't show them bailing on the club entirely about twenty minutes later. But he remembered those things every time he looked at the photo.

Stella touched the glass with the tip of her finger. "Why is it here, then?"

"Excuse me?"

Stella leveled those beautiful eyes at him. "It's been eight weeks. You haven't hung it yet."

"I really haven't gotten into the shop much."

It wasn't a lie, but it wasn't the truth, either. Because the truth was, every time he looked at Stella's bright eyes, he remembered the feeling of her lithe body in his arms, the way she'd lowered herself onto him with a ferocity that had blown his mind, the way she'd curled into his chest after the first time, her wicked grin all the more wicked with sated knowledge.

It should have been just sex. Great sex, but just sex. However, in the course of one evening, he'd found himself matching wits with a cultured, refined woman who subtly pushed his boundaries while she made him laugh. He'd been with a lot of women, but none had made him feel like Stella had. It was something he couldn't quite explain, not even to himself. When he was with another woman—any other woman, now that he thought about it—they were there to have a good time, but also…because he could offer them something—a little PR, another good tweet. But Stella hadn't been interested in mutual promotion and satisfaction. She'd been interested in *him*.

If he'd hung the photo on the wall in the shop, mixed in with all the other photos of famous people—some of whom he'd also slept with—then that would have meant that she was just like all the rest of them.

And she wasn't.

"Dinner's getting cold," was all he could say.

He held her chair for her. By the time he'd settled into his own chair, close enough to touch her, she was half done with the omelet. "This is excellent," she told him after she washed down another bite with coffee.

"Glad you liked it. Have you had a lot of morning sickness?"

Still chewing, she shrugged. "Some. The flight out…" She grimaced, her hand fluttering over her waist.

He nodded in sympathy. "Have you seen a doctor?"

She paused, as if she wanted to retreat behind that icy silence she'd first confronted him with. Then her shoulders relaxed. The bacon seemed to help. "Yes, two weeks ago. I'm eight weeks along, due on June 24."

A date—even one in the middle of next year—was

something concrete and real. All he could do was stare at his coffee as he repeated the date in his head. June 24. The date he'd be a father.

This was really happening.

"What do you want?"

It wasn't until the words were out that he realized he'd said them.

They were the wrong words—too much of an ultimatum—but he couldn't take them back. He'd spent approximately seven total hours in the company of Stella Caine. Seven hours wasn't long enough to base the rest of his life on.

Plus, she was David Caine's daughter. All of Bobby's plans—the television show, the destination resort, the chance to finally prove himself to his family? David Caine could change all of that, if he saw fit. This wasn't just about Bobby and Stella. This was something that affected the entire Bolton family.

He felt the icy wall Stella put up between them even before she set down her fork. She stood and walked across the room, the distance between them growing.

"It's not about what I want, not anymore." She looked out the patio door that led to a small balcony. "I won't complain about the lot I've drawn, but if I have this child, I need certain assurances about her future."

If.

So maybe Bobby wasn't ready to be a father. He might never actually be ready.

But he was a Bolton, by God, and there was one thing the Bolton men valued above all else—family. His father had married his mother when they were both seventeen, after Mom had gotten pregnant with Billy. Through the ups and downs of twenty-five years of marriage and motorcycles, the family had always come first.

If Bobby was going to be a father to Stella's child, then she was already family. For it to be any other way was unthinkable. Stella was giving him a chance to do the right thing here. He just had to man up and...

Marry her.

Make sure the baby was a Bolton, through and through.

This realization hit him harder than any punch ever had. Honest to God, his knees went weak and his vision blurred. *Married.* Oh, hell.

Stella was still staring out the window, thankfully. She hadn't seen his reaction. But she was probably expecting a reasonable response.

"What kind of assurances?"

He saw her reflection in the glass take a deep breath, but that was the only outward sign of her mental state. Otherwise, she was an unreadable wall.

"I will not have a child who is used as a pawn or a child who is not loved by her father. I'd rather she never know you exist than that she live life knowing she wasn't wanted."

That statement hung out there, practically icing over the glass with its frostiness. Something in the way she said it hit Bobby in a different way.

David Caine was world famous for being conservative— a staunch proponent of abstinence-only education, marriage between one man and one woman and no abortions—not even in cases of rape or incest. He believed in these rules and others so that when Bobby had signed on the dotted line for *The Bolton Biker Boys,* he'd also agreed to an extensive morals clause. David Caine believed there was such a thing as bad publicity, apparently, and he enforced a strict rule of law on what constituted "bad publicity." Which included almost everything that would land a man on TMZ or any other gossip site.

Which included getting his daughter pregnant out of wedlock.

Not that this particular situation was outlined in the contract, but Bobby had a feeling David Caine would do a

whole lot more than just terminate Bobby's contract with
FreeFall TV. He thought of Mickey, who still had Bobby's
Glock. Hell, he'd be lucky if David Caine didn't terminate
him, period.

He didn't like the distance she'd put between them, the
cold words she'd just said. It wasn't as if he wanted her sobbing and hysterical, but this detachment? *No.* He wasn't
having any of it.

So they barely knew each other. So this development
could blow all of his carefully laid plans to bits, probably
hers, as well. That didn't change the facts—they'd met, felt
an instant chemistry and followed up on it. He hadn't been
able to hang her picture on the wall with all the others.

He hadn't been able to stop thinking about her.

No, the one thing he knew was that she'd been wrong
in the back of her car, when she'd kissed him instead of
giving him her number and told him it was better this way.

Her way was not better.

Time to try it his way.

He went to her, folded her into his arms and kissed the
spot on the back of her neck.

Her skin was cool against his lips, her body ramrod stiff
in his arms. She was going to fight him on this, fight to
maintain her icy detachment. *I don't think so,* he thought
as he kissed his way around her neck until he got to that
special spot, the one just below her ear, half hidden by a
silver earring. When he traced the area with his tongue,
she shuddered.

For a brief moment, her back arched. Her bottom pushed
against him. *Yes,* he thought. *Unleash that energy on me.*

But then she pulled away from him and said, "Stop."

Bobby froze. But he didn't let her go. Instead, he held
her even tighter, hoping the steel would leave her body. He
let his hands skim over her body until they rested on her
stomach. Between the leather bodice of her dress and the
fact that she wasn't very far along, he would never have

guessed she was pregnant. But if she'd already seen a doctor, then it was a fact.

He felt the smooth plane of her body—a body that held his child. "Is that what you want? This baby to never know my name? To never know that I loved her?"

She sucked in a hard breath, as if Bobby had slapped her. "This isn't about what I want," she said again. But she didn't sound as if she believed it. "This is about what's best for everyone involved."

Damn it, he was done with her forced detachment. They weren't discussing stock options or a merger or whatever she and her father talked about around the dinner table. This was a life—a baby-to-be—theirs.

Careful not to hurt her, he turned her in his arms as he backed her up against the glass doors. Although she moved, her body was not the soft, welcoming thing he dreamed of at night.

She refused to meet his gaze, though, so once he had her secure, he lifted her chin until she looked him in the eyes. No mistaking it this time—she was terrified of what he might say. "I don't care what 'everyone' thinks is best. I only care about what you want."

He saw the doubt flash over her eyes right before she shut them. "It's better this way."

She sounded as though she was on the verge of tears, but Bobby didn't care. He wanted to know that she cared—one way or the other.

"Better for who?"

He kissed her, just a touch of two lips.

Just a promise.

Then, in a flash, the cold steel melted from her body. She laced her arms around his neck and pulled him down as her mouth opened, her tongue hesitantly tracing his lips.

He couldn't deny it. He needed her.

He hadn't really stopped needing her, not since that night two months ago. She hadn't been far from his mind, despite the long hours and the crazy schedule and the determination that everything would be perfect.

As she warmed against him, his body responded. For every degree she softened, he got that much harder, that much hotter, until his skin was on fire, desperate to feel hers against him.

It had not been an accident, the first time. The chemistry between them was electric, shocking him again with how strong it was. He wanted to bury himself in her body, to feel the force of her desire unleashed on him again.

Except he had no idea how to get her out of this dress.

He pulled back. Desire warmed her features and she looked up at him through thick black eyelashes. Oh, yeah, that was the woman he'd lost himself in two months ago—sensual, witty, aware of the power she held over him and not afraid to give him a little power over her.

God, he was so glad she was here. He wanted to keep her here—if he didn't, she might slip away from him and he didn't think he could handle that a second time.

He kissed her again, letting his tongue trace her lips—tasting what he'd missed. He'd missed her in a way that didn't make a damn bit of sense. He never got involved. He'd never wanted a relationship—certainly had never wanted to be a father.

But something about her…

Her cell phone chirped from somewhere on the other side of the room. "Sorry," she murmured as she moved away from him. "Mickey."

Yeah, he'd sort of forgotten about the leprechaun.

Stella retrieved her cell phone from her coat pocket. "Yes? Yes. No."

Bobby couldn't hear both sides of the conversation, but he could guess. Mickey was somewhere nearby, waiting for the word to come in, shoot Bobby in the knee and swoop Stella away. Okay, so maybe he wouldn't shoot Bobby—but he was here for Stella, one way or the other.

Bobby wasn't ready for her to leave just yet.

He approached her, hand out for her phone. "May I?"

The look she gave him was almost comical—doubtful and confused and cold and yet still very much tinged with the desire that had reddened her lips.

"I just want to talk to him for a minute."

"Yes—he's here. He wants to talk." Then she handed Bobby the phone.

"Keeping yer cool up there, laddie?"

Bobby gritted out a smile. "We're doing well, thanks for asking. I've been thinking. I don't know where Stella is staying, but if she's coming and going at a hotel, the media might pick up on that. They might try to make a story out of it."

"Is that so," Mickey said in such a way that Bobby turned to glance out the patio doors, just to make sure the man wasn't sitting on his small deck, weapon drawn.

"Yes. Perhaps it would be better for Stella's long-term well-being if she stayed in a more secure location, at least through the weekend."

Stella gave him a look—one eyebrow raised, lips pursed— that only made him want to kiss her again.

"Are ye speaking the queen's English?"

Bobby grinned at Stella. "I think you should stay here for the weekend."

"What?" Stella said.

"What?" Mickey echoed in his ear.

Bobby ignored Mickey. "Stay here with me," he said to Stella. "Just until we can decide what's best for everyone involved."

"Oh." Stella's eyes were as wide as the moon.

"Saints help us all, *that* part I understood," Mickey muttered. "Let me talk to me girl again."

That last bit—*me girl*—struck Bobby as odd, but he didn't press the issue. What Mickey needed in this negotiation was to know that he had fulfilled his duty to protect Stella. Anything Bobby did that cast doubt on her well-being was, more than likely, a permanent black mark against him.

"Absolutely." He handed the phone back over, but he didn't move out of earshot. Instead, he reached down and took Stella's free hand in his.

"No, I didn't—but it's okay. Yes. Yes. If you think it'll be all right…" She squeezed Bobby's hand. "Fine." She ended the call. "He'll be by with my things." The nervous look stole over her face again.

Bobby understood. After all, she'd just agreed to what had the potential to be a highly intimate weekend with someone who was little more than a stranger. "I'll sleep on the couch."

"I don't want to put you out."

But he could see by the look on her face that she was pleased he wasn't pinning her against a wall and giving her no choice. Sort of like he'd done about ten minutes ago. And a lot like he wanted to do right now.

"It's not a problem. But there's still a lot we need to talk about. Right now, I only know a few things. I know that I met you eight weeks ago, that there was something between us—something good. I know that I haven't been able to get you out of my mind since then. I know that I'm glad to see you. I know that your father doesn't know where you are and that we both want to keep it that way until we have a plan. I know you sew and make your own lace. But beyond that—"

He leaned forward, brushing the sharp angle of hair away from her cheekbone, marveling at the pale blush that sprang up wherever his fingertips touched. She could pretend that she was some sort of ice princess, but he knew better. Buried beneath her cold detachment was a woman whose blood ran as hot as his did.

"Beyond that, I don't know you like I need to. That's what I want to work on this weekend."

This time, she didn't look away, didn't close her eyes. She met his gaze straight on. "What if it takes more than a weekend?"

If the baby was his, then they had all the time in the world. For Bolton men, family came first. Family was everything. Of course, he hadn't quite figured out how that was going to work while he built a resort, produced a reality show and helped run a company.

That's why he needed the weekend. That, and he wanted to keep her as close to him as possible.

He grinned and was rewarded with a smile that got so, so close to wicked. "Then we'll make a damn good start."

Four

Bobby drew her a bath. At first, Stella had scoffed when he'd offered to fill up the tub. But he'd done so, anyway, insisting that she should relax.

So here she sat, nude, stretched out in a tub that had jets. The water covered her body, the warmth seeping into her bones. The whole time, she was thinking, *What am I doing?*

Because taking a warm bath, sleeping in Bobby Bolton's bed—even if he wasn't in it with her—was not the plan. Although, with her stomach happily full and the bath doing an admirable job of making her sleepy, she was having trouble remembering what, exactly, the plan had been. Show up. Inform him of his contribution to her situation. Determine if he would be supportive of the child or not. Decide what she was going to do. Go home.

Alone.

But this? Soaking her toes in his bath? Sleeping in his very large bed? Eating the meal that he'd made for her? Seeing the photo of the two of them so prominently displayed on his table?

Feeling as if he *cared* for her?

No. How he made her feel—as if she was more than just an inconvenience to be dealt with, more than just a reminder of a painful mistake he'd made—this was a short-lived sensation and could not figure into her plans. It wouldn't last. Aside from Mickey, bless his soul, no man had ever done a thing to take care of her. She had no reason to think that Bobby was any different. Not once the shock of the situation wore off, anyway.

Stella cradled her belly with her hands. She couldn't tell if her body had changed—not on the outside, anyway. Inside, she was something of a mess.

Her world was carefully controlled to buffer her against the slings and arrows of outrageous fortune. Because she couldn't bear another arrow. Better to feel nothing than to feel the pain that had been her constant companion since her mum's death.

But Bobby…she felt things for Bobby. That was how she'd gotten into this fine mess in the first place—he made her feel things that she'd never felt before. Happy. Exuberant. Silly, even. She'd laughed with him in the club when he'd told a disparaging story about his brother breaking his jaw, and she'd giggled in his arms in the back of the car, and the orgasm she'd experienced brought forth a whole new range of feelings.

Now she was feeling *things,* things that she didn't want to feel, because feelings were messy and unclear and hard to control.

She hadn't lied to Bobby. She wouldn't allow him to use the child as a pawn in negotiations with her father. Better that her baby never knew her father, if that's how it was going to be. At least, that had been the plan. The life she had was not a life she wanted to pass on to another generation.

From far away, she heard a knock. A loud, insistent knock. She knew immediately it was Mickey. *Good ol' Mick,* she thought, he'd always taken care of her—maybe not in a motherly way, but God knows, the man had put his heart into it.

Still lost in that space between awake and dreaming, she heard Bobby say something she couldn't quite make out. Then, loudly, Mickey said, "I want to talk to me girl meself, if ye don't mind."

That, coupled with the approaching sounds of men jostling for position, snapped Stella out of her daze. Mickey would bully his way into the bedroom and—if she wasn't careful—the bathroom. He was a great many things, but sensible about these sorts of situations he wasn't.

But instead of an old man bursting in on her in the bath, she heard a gentle knock on the door. "Stella? Mickey's here with your things and he'd like to have a word with you. There should be a robe hanging on the back of the door."

"Yes, one moment." Reluctantly, she stood.

It was a nice bathrobe, the soft, luxe kind that had probably cost a lot of money. But that wasn't what Stella liked about it. What she liked was how, as she slipped it over her still-damp shoulders, the smell of Gucci by Gucci wrapped around her, as warm and inviting as the robe itself. Bobby had worn that scent at the club. She hadn't realized how much that smell had remained with her.

Outside, she could hear Mickey's grumbling getting louder. She quickly ran a towel over her damp hair, destroying what was left of her perfect bob. Ah, well. Tomorrow she'd do it up proper.

When she opened the door, she was surprised to see Bobby standing in the doorway to the hall. "I'll leave you two alone," was all he said, but before the door shut, Stella saw the cheeky wink he shot at her. Mickey didn't scare him. Not much, anyway.

"How ye feeling?" Mickey waved at the two bags set on the end of the bed. "There's all yer things."

"Thank you."

It always amazed Stella how much more English her accent became when it was just her and Mickey. Most of the time, when she was in New York, she hardly heard the notes of Britain in her voice at all. But when it was just her and Mickey—even if they were in an unfamiliar bedroom—everything came out thicker.

Mickey heard it, too. His eyes softened. "Ye sound like yer dear mum, lass."

She'd heard that before, too—Mickey was fond of noting it—but this time, it hit her funny. Her eyes began to water as she placed a hand over her stomach. She knew the babe was still too tiny to feel, months would pass before her whole body began to twitch with small kicks, but still...

God bless Mickey for trying, but what she really wanted was a mother—someone who'd fold Stella into her arms and hold her as she cried about this strange situation she found herself in. A mother would be able to answer all of Stella's questions about the baby inside her with that wonderful phrase "When I was pregnant with you..." A mother would reassure her that everything would turn out, just wait and see.

That was something she'd never had and never would. Which had probably led her to where she was today—in a world of trouble.

"Oh, now," Mickey said in his gruff way, fishing out a worn kerchief from his back pocket and handing it to her. "Don't start with that."

"It's fine," was all she could say, waving off the kerchief. Even though it wasn't.

Mickey eyed her before he accepted the dodge. This is what they did, after all. Danced up to the edge of emotions before waltzing in the other direction. "Are ye sure you should stay with *him?* Is that the best idea?"

"He said he'd sleep on the sofa."

"Pshaw." Mickey tapped his toe. This was also part of their normal routine. Mickey stridently stated his opinions—ranging from her modeling jobs to her outfit choices—and then acquiesced to what Stella wanted. That night at the club, eight weeks ago? Mickey hadn't thought it was a good idea to go to the party. He'd thought it an even worse idea to slip into the backseat of the car. But instead of stopping Stella from making the single biggest mistake of her life, he'd stood guard so that no one interrupted them.

Really, Mickey was a huge softy underneath that crusty exterior.

"Suppose it's not like he could get ye more pregnant than you already are." Stella shot him a look that made the old man blush. "I still say that we don't need him. Just ol' Mick, Lala and the wee one. We'll manage just fine, the three of us."

Lala. It'd been her childhood name for herself, when she couldn't get the *St* sound just right. Her mother had called her Lala, too.

Her father had never called her Lala. Not once.

How different would it have been if Mickey had been Stella's father? After all, it was no lie to say the two men had been friends since the day they were born. Mickey Roberts and David Caine had been born on the same day in the same hospital in Dublin. They'd gone to Campbell College in Belfast together. They'd been joyriding in David's car together when they'd seen Claire O'Flannery coming out of a church one summer afternoon. The only difference was that David Caine came from an old family with older money and Mickey Roberts had scraped by on scholarships and sheer luck.

David had never forgotten his oldest friend. Mickey had worked as David's driver-slash-bodyguard as David had dramatically expanded the Caine family holdings into media, mobile and whatever mergers he could make.

Including merging with Claire O'Flannery. Not even the Catholic schoolgirl, just past her nineteenth birthday, had been able to resist David Caine—or the money that went with him.

Mickey would take care of Stella's baby as best he could, just as he'd taken care of her. But he was sixty now, more set in his ways than he liked to admit. Despite his best efforts to stand in as both a mother and a father, he wasn't a natural at either role. Stella loved her old friend, but she couldn't picture him changing a nappy. At least, not without a fair amount of curse words.

"We've been over this, Mickey. It's his child, too. He gets to have a say."

"Hmmph." Mickey shot a mean look at the door. "I don't like him. Too smooth."

"You don't like anyone."

This was a fact. Except usually, Mickey was proven right. He hadn't liked Brian, her last paramour—and that relationship had ended when Stella had refused to invite her father over for dinner so that Brian could pitch his Great Big Idea to a captive audience. Mickey hadn't liked Neil before that—too much eye makeup, not enough backbone. Which explained how Neil had left her in the middle of a questionable club while he chased an easier skirt.

She hoped that wasn't what Bobby was about. Somehow, it felt like a blanket denial, followed quickly by a general refusal to accept the baby, would be easier to take than to find out that he'd been more interested in finding an in with her father from the beginning.

Mickey scuffed a toe on the carpet. He was bending. He always did. "Said I could sleep on the couch, he did."

She thought of the way Bobby had touched her face in the car park, the way he'd pinned her against the glass in the living room. She breathed in the scent of his cologne and snuggled deeper into his plush robe. Bobby *was* too smooth. But that didn't change the situation. Smoothness had no impact on pregnancy. Except to occasionally cause it.

She loved Mickey, she did—but she didn't need a chaperone. She was a grown woman of twenty-five, carrying a baby. Plus, she knew Mickey's weakness—room service.

"No, I don't think that's necessary."

Mickey glared at her, but she could see him thinking about dessert delivered to his door. "Ye keep yer mobile next to ye, hear? Ye call me at any time, fer any reason."

"Of course. But this is something I have to figure out for myself."

"I suppose…" Mickey let out a heavy sigh. Stella smiled at him. Stubborn until the very end. "He lays a hand on ye, though, and all bets are off."

"It'll be fine," she promised.

She just wished she believed it.

Bobby stared at his phone. He'd been tempted to listen in on Stella's conversation with the leprechaun, but he had something to do.

Man, he didn't want to make this call. But he didn't have much choice. With Stella's presence in his condo, there was no shot in hell that he'd meet all of his deadlines.

So he braced for the worst.

"It's late," Ben said. But the fact that he'd answered on the first ring told Bobby that his older brother had been at his desk, not in bed.

"I know. I have a problem."

Even saying those words out loud was a blow to Bobby's ego, but having to say them to Ben? Mr. Responsible himself? Ben would never let him live this down. And it wasn't just that he was missing a deadline. It was that he'd gotten Stella pregnant. Family was everything to the Bolton boys. The moment he told any member of his family that he was a father-to-be was the moment he lost any illusion of control over his own life.

"What?" Ben snapped.

"I'm not going to make the sales projection deadline."

"Damn it, Bobby. I have that meeting with the bank."

"I know, I know." He wasn't good at feeling guilty. It made him uncomfortable. "I have an unexpected house-guest."

"This better not be some girl crashing at your place."

When Bobby didn't say anything, he heard a noise that might have been Ben throwing the phone. He couldn't tell.

After a moment, Ben got back on the phone. His voice was lower, but much more pissed. "You're telling me you're going to miss a deadline because of some woman?"

Bobby swallowed. Ben was a backer on the resort, but he'd chipped in only after his wife had strong-armed him. "Is Josey still up?"

"What?"

"Josey. Your wife. Is she still awake? I need to talk to her."

"She's in bed. Callie's got another ear infection. I've got the night shift tonight. What the hell does that have to do with you missing the deadline because you picked up some chick?"

Bobby took a deep breath, trying to hear if Mickey and Stella were heading out of the bedroom. Nothing. He had a few minutes left to talk, but not much more than that.

He didn't want to do this, but what choice did he have? Ben, after all, was a father. Someone he could ask for advice. Someone who would know what to do next.

"My houseguest is also—" The words hit the back of his teeth, refusing to budge. Saying them out loud made it more real. "She's pregnant."

Ben didn't say anything, which was sort of a mixed blessing. On the one hand, he wasn't calling Bobby a jerk or a twit or telling him how bad he'd messed up.

On the other hand, the weight of Ben's silence felt as if someone had dropped a massive oak tree on Bobby's chest and was in no hurry to lift it off.

Finally, Ben said, "Yours?"

"That's what she says."

"Make sure it's yours. Then do the right damn thing, Robert."

"Then I guess I shouldn't have called you, should I?"

"Twit," Ben muttered. "You know what I mean."

"Look, I'm sorry about the projections. But this is more important."

"Fine." That was the nice thing about Ben. After he got it out of his system, he was able to focus on the business at hand. Billy, the oldest Bolton, probably would have driven over here to beat Bobby to a pulp. "You want me to wake Josey?"

That seemed like a colossally bad idea, especially if she was already tired. "No, let her sleep. Will she be around this weekend?"

"Yeah. I'll have her call you." Ben paused. "You've got to make this right."

Bobby knew what that meant. Family, Dad liked to say, was everything. This baby-to-be would be a Bolton. He and Stella had to get married, for better or for worse.

"I will," he promised his brother.

He hung up just as the bedroom door opened. Mickey came out, looking cranky. "Should I make up a pallet on the couch for you?"

"That won't be necessary."

Stella emerged from behind Mickey, wrapped in Bobby's robe, her hair still mussed from the bath.

Enchanting, he thought as she looked up at him through thick lashes. Everything about her seemed softer, more touchable. Did she have anything on underneath the robe? Probably not. Boy, did he ever want to touch her.

"Ahem," Mickey coughed, spreading his legs wide and standing between Bobby and Stella.

Right. Humoring the old man. "Are you sure? Plenty of room. No trouble at all."

With an impressive eye roll, Mickey looked back to Stella, who said, "Thanks, but Mickey will be more comfortable back at the hotel."

"Aye," Mickey agreed, although he didn't seem happy about this. "But I'm watching you." He turned and patted Stella on the cheek. "Take care o' yerself, lass."

Stella smiled as she leaned down and kissed him on the

cheek. "Don't eat too many ice lollies, hear?" Her voice was different when she said this—richer, more rolling.

Despite the worry and the late hour and the completely surreal nature of the evening, Bobby's blood ran hot. This Stella was much closer to the woman who'd let loose in the back of a car—no stiff clothing, no detached attitude.

He wanted to take her back to bed, peel that robe off her and bury himself deep in her body. He wanted to hear her cry out his name again—that was what he'd wanted ever since the first time.

But he'd promised. He'd sleep on the couch, if that was what she wanted.

He *had* to make this right.

Pretty darned hard to do from the couch.

Five

The couch was not a comfortable place to sleep.

Bobby had this epiphany around two in the morning as he tried to figure out what the hell to do with his feet. He needed a longer couch, for starters, and one that had less metal in the armrests. Finally, he gave up, threw his pillow on the floor and tried to enjoy being flat.

The lack of bedding wasn't the only thing that kept him from sleep. It was the thought of how, after Mickey had finally taken his leave, Bobby and Stella had stood right over there, staring at each other. Bobby had wanted to pull her into his arms and kiss her, but she'd looked so sweet, so vulnerable that he hadn't been able to move.

The best he had been able to do was to ask, "Can I get you anything?"

She'd replied, "Thanks, no. The bath was lovely, but I'm rather tired."

"Of course." It had been fast approaching midnight.

Stella had gone back into his bedroom—alone—and shut the door. Bobby had made do on an instrument of torture masquerading as a couch.

How was he going to make this right? Or, more to the point, how did Stella want him to make this right? She'd given no sign that she wanted to get married—this despite having one of the most world-famous supporters of heterosexual marriage for a father.

She just wanted assurances. *Certain* assurances. Whatever those were.

Finally, he gave up on sleep and turned his attention to a problem he could actually solve. Stella was eating for two now. Sure, he'd cobbled together a decent meal late last night, but he didn't have enough supplies on hand to get them through a weekend. So he got up, wrote out a list of things he hoped she'd like and left a note with his cell phone number next to the photo of them.

The nice thing about shopping at six-thirty on a Saturday morning was that the store was essentially empty. He loaded his cart up with staples. The whole time, he thought. Easier to think when he was picking apples than when he was on the floor.

Stella was pregnant. He was most likely the father. He needed to marry her. That was the only way to make it right—to make sure the baby was a Bolton. It was the only way to be sure Stella wouldn't disappear with another "it's better this way."

The specter of David Caine hovered at the edge of Bobby's thoughts. Sooner or later, the owner of FreeFall TV would find out that his newest reality star had impregnated his only daughter. Sooner or later, the executive producer of *The Bolton Biker Boys* would know that Bobby had broken every known morals clause of a legally binding contract and possibly a few unknown ones.

How was he supposed to make things right with Stella when her father would likely drag him to court for breaking his contract? How would he take care of his family—his father, his brothers *and* Stella and the baby—without the resort? To a certain point, he didn't care about the reality show. It was just the vehicle to get him the financing to make the resort a success. Maybe the world wouldn't end if Caine canceled the show—but if Caine pulled out of the resort, too?

How would Bobby take care of his family then?

Eventually, Bobby couldn't fit anything else into the cart. In the check-out line, he spotted the floral displays. On impulse, he grabbed a mixed bouquet. He'd make French toast for breakfast. A quiche for lunch would be good, with some baked broccoli and a salad. Then for dinner—well, he'd wait to see what Stella wanted.

He was aware he was avoiding the real issues, as if solving the food problem was the most important thing right now. But he couldn't help it. Planning meals was a problem with a definable, achievable solution.

He trucked hundreds of dollars' worth of groceries home. Somehow, he got everything into the apartment without waking Stella. Eight came and went. Bobby made the quiche, then began marinating the filets, just in case she was in the mood for steak. He found a recipe for pumpkin muffins and roasted a pumpkin.

Soon enough, the kitchen smelled fabulous, which buoyed his mood considerably. Cooking always made him feel better. The kitchen had been a quiet, warm place in his childhood. Dad and Billy—Ben, too—had always been out racing bikes or arguing or making a general mess of things, but the kitchen had been Mom's domain. Hats off at the table, hands and faces washed, pleases and thank-yous all around—enforced with a wooden spoon. Even Dad, crusty old fart that he was, had bowed to these rules of civility. At the table, they were a family, no matter what else was happening outside. Bobby had learned how to get people to do what he wanted from his mother, no shouting required.

Then a thought hit him. When was the last time he'd cooked for a woman? Hell—when was the last time he'd had a woman sleep the whole night in his bed?

There'd been Marla, in Beverly Hills. She'd been fun and energetic and beautiful and *very* well connected. They'd made a habit of hooking up whenever he was in town, which had progressed to spending the whole night together. It had almost felt like a relationship.

Then he'd made her breakfast one morning—at her place. Even put a rose on the tray. Hands down, it was the most romantic thing he'd ever done.

And Marla had...well, not laughed at him. She would never be so tactless as that. But instead of being impressed, she'd been amused. *Confused.* Why would a man like Bobby make her breakfast? He thought he'd been doing something special for her, and she thought he'd been silly. He wouldn't lie. It had stung like hell.

The relationship ended fairly quickly after that. That had been four years ago. He hadn't seen the same woman more than twice since then. He'd told himself he liked it that way. Everyone knew up front that things were a one-night-only special—a little fun, a little sex, no strings attached.

Just as it had been with Stella.

Except he'd asked her for her number. Bobby paused in the middle of chopping the broccoli. Now that he thought about it, when was the last time he'd asked a woman for something *after* sex? For something more?

Not since Marla.

Stella had said no then. No strings attached. That's the way he'd always operated and it had always worked just fine. Of course, he'd never experienced this kind of connection with a woman before.

Stella had been ghosting around the edge of his thoughts for months now, but he'd honored her wishes. He hadn't contacted her. Even though she had driven him to distraction.

Now the strings that bound them were most definitely attached.

It was almost too much to think about. So he made French toast instead.

Finally, breakfast was ready—and Stella had still not emerged. Bobby looked at the clock. Nine in the morning. He should wake her up.

For a moment, he wanted to get the food plated up, put

a stem or two in a small vase and bring her breakfast in bed. But the memory of Marla's lip curling stopped him. He didn't want another woman to look at him so dismissively.

After he made sure all the burners on the stove were off, he knocked on the bedroom door. "Stella?"

Nothing.

He opened the door a crack. Even though the sun came up late, it was still plenty bright enough in the room. "Stella?"

She was on her back, one arm dramatically thrown over her head and the covers all pushed down around her waist. Her hair was a tousled mass of black and she was wearing a thin little camisole.

A thin little camisole that had shifted.

The sight of her breast bared sent a spike of heat through Bobby. He'd seen her before, of course, but that was different. They'd been tipsy and turned on and she'd stripped her belted dress off as if she'd had something to prove.

This was another thing entirely. How could she look so soft, so sweet?

No. *No.* Bobby slammed the brakes on those thoughts. He was not the kind of guy who woke up a woman he barely knew by seducing her, even if she was in his bed and they had had sex once. Well, technically twice.

"Stella?"

She shifted, which only revealed more of her creamy skin—skin his hands were itching to touch.

Memories of her body consuming his came crashing back through his mind. The power of her desire—the way she'd grabbed his hands and held him down—had been a kind of erotic that he never wanted to forget.

A kind of erotic that he wanted to have again.

"Stella." It was more of a plea this time—he needed her to wake up, to cover up, to stop him before he did something incredibly stupid, like kiss her awake.

"Hmm." Her other arm flopped up, stretching her body out. And pulling the camisole even lower.

Now both nipples were exposed to the morning light. Bobby closed his eyes.

Then he became aware that his feet were moving, walking him toward the bed. Toward her. He couldn't seem to stop himself. His feet knew the way. He didn't need his eyes to find her.

I'm in trouble.

"Stella, darling," he whispered as he knelt down beside the bed. He opened his eyes long enough to grab the comforter and pull it up over her chest. "It's past nine. Time to get up."

"Mmph." She shifted and suddenly they were face to face. Her eyes were the palest of greens in this light. He'd never seen eyes like hers before. One of a kind. Just like Stella.

"Oh," she breathed as she blinked at him. "Hi."

"Morning." Then he heard himself add, "Beautiful."

A sleepy smile curved her lips into a sweetheart bow—a kissable bow. Then one of the hands that had been flung over her head came down and she rested her palm on his cheek. He hadn't shaved.

Her touch was cool but it made his blood run hot. He was *not* touching her. That was final. He was a gentleman.

"I made you breakfast."

Her fingers stiffened against his skin, but she wasn't pushing him away. If anything, it felt as if she was tightening against him. "You made me…breakfast?"

The way she said it—breathless and surprised and, underneath all of that, *pleased*—turned his temperature up another notch.

"Yup. French toast." Then a new thought occurred to him. "Is that okay? I didn't think—with you being British…"

She giggled, a small, delicate sound that danced like

bells over Bobby's ears. "You made breakfast. For me," she repeated.

As she said it, her hand slipped back through his hair until she was cupping the back of his head. Until she was pulling him forward.

"Yeah." All he could see was the breathless way she was looking at him. "I wanted to make it right. I *want* to make it right." He'd sort of thought that he was talking about breakfast, but that last part? Not about food.

The next thing Bobby knew, Stella was kissing him— not the kind of kiss that said "thank you for the meal." Oh, no. This was the kind of kiss that had Bobby clutching the comforter, hanging on to his self-control by a thread. A fraying thread.

That thread snapped when Stella's tongue traced his lips. He'd behaved honorably here. He hadn't started this.

But he'd finish it, by God.

He pulled the comforter back down, revealing her bare breasts. The sight of her body made him ache in ways he hadn't known were possible. "Beautiful," he breathed again, which made her gasp in surprise. Hadn't anyone ever told her that before?

Maybe they had. She had done some modeling, he knew. But maybe she'd never believed it.

Keeping his eyes on hers—so wide with desire and need—he cupped her breast and stroked his way up from the side to the stiff peak of her nipple.

It was so hard to go slow, to wait and see what her re-action would be. He was straining behind the half-undone zipper. He didn't want slow and he wasn't sold on gentle— he wanted the same frenzied sex they'd had last time.

But it was worth the wait as she sucked in another hot breath, her fingers digging into the back of his head. Yeah, she liked that. He stroked her breast again. This time, he got a moan out of her. She was going to kill him, plain and simple, and he wanted nothing more than to die in her arms.

He lowered his mouth onto her breast. He licked at the delicate underside, working his way up to what had become an incredibly pointed nipple. Stella had both hands buried in his hair, holding him to her as he focused on making this right.

"Oh, yes," she said, her accent crisp even though she was now breathing heavily. He found the contrast amusing.

"Mmm," was all he said as he teased her nipple. Her skin tasted as creamy as it looked, with a hint of sweetness underneath. Peaches and cream, he thought as he slid his hands under the comforter, pushing it back until he revealed a thin pair of white panties, all silk and lace.

So delicate, so feminine. So *beautiful*. He slipped his hands underneath the waist of her panties, palming her backside underneath the silk and tasting her other breast.

He wanted to make this right for *her*.

His hands were shaking with the effort of restraining himself. Normally, Bobby was able to remain above the intimacy of a sexual encounter—he enjoyed the women he slept with, but he never got attached, *never* lost his cool.

She did this to him in a way that no other woman ever had.

At this moment, more than anything, he just needed *her*.

He pulled the pointless camisole off over her head as she fumbled with his jeans. Somehow, he wound up on the bed, half under the covers. Stella jerked at his shirt, which didn't make it over his head. Even though he still had his pants down around his ankles—even though she still had on those lace panties—he couldn't wait to kiss her again. He lowered himself onto her, loving the way her arms slipped around his waist, the way her nails dug into his back with just enough pressure to let him know that she wanted him as much as he wanted her.

He took her mouth with a white-hot kiss, tasting the noises of need she made in the back of her throat. This is

what had kept him up at night over the past two months—
this feeling that something about Stella was different.

She deserved his very best. It was his duty to give it
to her.

Her back arched into him, pushing the warmth of her
center, barely contained by those damn panties, into him.
Bobby groaned at the pressure that spiked through him.

At the last possible second—as he pulled her panties
aside—he remembered the condom. He always wore one.
Out of habit, he leaned over and snagged one out of the
drawer on his bedside table, rolled it on with expert preci-
sion and turned back to the woman in his bed. The whole
process took seconds.

Which was just long enough for a shadow of doubt to
take up residence on Stella's face.

"Do you want me to stop?"

She bit her lip, which made it that much redder. Damn
it, holding himself back when she was so beautiful, so open
before him, was an agony unlike anything he'd ever experienced before. He *would* stop, if she said to. But then he'd
probably wind up punching a wall or something.

Her hands against his chest went from pushing against
him to pulling on him—pulling him down to her. Bobby
let her. His erection found her wet center all on its own.

As her body took him in, he leaned back so he could
watch her. Her mouth opened, but no noise came out. Her
eyes were closed, but once he was all the way in, her eye-
lids fluttered and she looked up at him through thick lashes.

"Beautiful," he murmured as he stared into the pale jade
she called eyes. So cool on the surface, but so very much
going on underneath.

He sealed the deal with another kiss as he began to rock
in and out of her. The way her body tightened around his—
the way she dragged her nails down his back—everything
about being with Stella was better.

"Do you like it like this?"

"Yes, quite— *Oh!*"

Over and over, he thrust into her—over and over, she made that little *oh!* noise. Finally, he couldn't take it anymore. He kissed her, hard, swallowing up the sound of her pleasure as his body released the climax.

She hadn't come yet—damn it. He would *not* leave her behind. He grabbed her hands and held them against the pillow. Stella's body tried to curl into a ball—the opposite of arching—as her wrists strained under his hands. He remembered that from the first time—it had surprised him the way her body had tensed and curled up as she'd climaxed on top of him.

Then she unfurled, stretching out against his body as she moaned in pure pleasure. Bobby collapsed on top of her. He withdrew from her body and rolled onto his side, careful to pull the condom off and drop it in the trash can next to his bedside.

Then he pulled Stella's now-limp body into his arms. She made a noise that sounded like a feline purr as she nuzzled into his chest. Yeah, it had been hard to keep going, but it'd been worth it to take care of her.

Because that's what he was going to do.

He was going to take care of Stella.

Six

Bobby's arms tightened around Stella. His chest was warm and solid and very real. For a moment, she was afraid she'd dreamed waking up to find Bobby kneeling next to her. She had dreamed just such a thing, several times over—but this time it had been real.

He was really here. Making love to her in the morning. Making her breakfast, of all things.

She sighed and snuggled into him, enjoying the sensation of just *being*. How lovely that the first time hadn't just been the bubbly—that he really did make her feel this way.

"Lovely." She heard herself sigh.

A low chuckle rumbled out of Bobby's chest. "Can't wait to see what you do when I tell you what we're having for lunch." Then he kissed the top of her head.

Stella took stock of her stomach. So far, she didn't feel nauseated. She took a deep breath, trying to catch the scent of breakfast. But all she could smell was Bobby—the trace of the Gucci cologne mixed in with his own clean musk. "We'll start with breakfast."

"One meal at a time," he agreed.

She grinned up at him. He wasn't clean-shaven the way he normally was. In fact, he didn't look anything like the man she'd taken to her car. Everything that had formerly been smooth and polished about him was now rough.

"How was the couch?"

"Not good. The floor was only slightly better."

She feathered her hand over the fine smattering of blond hairs that covered his chest. His shirt was still partly on from their hurried lovemaking. "I do think it's no longer presumptuous of you to sleep in your own bed tonight."

He stretched against her. "Only one problem with that scenario."

"What's that?"

"You're assuming we'll sleep."

Stella felt her face grow hot, which was somewhat ridiculous, given that they were already sharing said bed.

Suddenly she wished that things were just like this. Him making her dinner, drawing her a bath, making love to her in the morning. Was it wrong to want that?

Of course it was wrong, she scolded herself. She clung to him for a moment longer, trying to store this warm memory away for when she'd need it later. Disregarding the current physical closeness, they still barely knew each other. Bobby Bolton was still too smooth, too charming. What happened when he turned that off? Would he use their child as a bargaining chip to wring what he wanted out of David Caine? Or would he sever himself from her, from their child—as her father had?

"Bobby?"

"Hmm?"

Stella swallowed, trying not to let her nerves get the best of her. "Why did you use a condom?" It's not as if she would be risking getting even more pregnant.

Bobby's chest rose and fell against hers. "When you went to the doctor, I'm assuming they ran all the tests on you—to rule out any illness or…diseases?"

"Yes. Because the sex was…" Random. Accidental. With a virtual stranger.

"I haven't gotten a physical since last January and I want to keep you safe." He kissed her forehead again, his lips lingering. "I haven't been with anyone else since that night with you."

Part of Stella absolutely melted at those words. She hadn't asked because she hadn't wanted to hear the answer. She'd forced herself to accept the fact that a man who went off with a woman at a bar would most likely do it more than once.

But he hadn't.

It almost felt as if he'd been waiting for her to show up here.

She shook some sense back into her head. Of course he hadn't been waiting on her. He was just making the most of an awkward situation.

"I need to make an appointment with my doctor, get tested again," Bobby said, stroking her hair away from her forehead. "And..."

Stella held very still. "And?"

"And I think we should have a paternity test done." He squeezed her tightly as he said it. "In a couple of months other people are going to notice you're pregnant. Including *your* father. Including *my* father. When we have test results in hand, then..."

Not bloody likely that David Caine would notice she was rounding out. He'd have to see her to notice *that*. The bitterness of this thought made Stella's heart hurt in ways that she didn't like to think about.

"Then?"

He took a deep breath, as if he was bracing for a hit. "Then we'll get married."

She blinked. And then she blinked again. But the view of his fine chest didn't change. So she dug her fingernails into her palm, hoping the pain would wake her up. After all, she'd had dreams of Bobby coming to her bedside. Clearly, this was just one of the more vivid ones.

Because it wasn't possible that he'd just asked her to marry him.

Her nails cut deep, almost breaking skin. The pain was a quick, unwelcome dose of reality.

Oh, bloody hell.

That wasn't why she'd come. She had no intention of trapping Bobby into a loveless marriage. But her heart had other ideas. Suddenly she saw the two of them living together, raising their baby—being a family. God, how she wanted that vision—the warmth, the closeness. The love. That, more than anything else in this life or the next, was what she needed—a family of her own. Somewhere she belonged, somewhere she was wanted. Somewhere that was hers.

Theirs.

Was that what he was talking about—a family, a real one? One where mothers and fathers loved not only each other but also their baby no matter what, through sickness and health, till death do them part?

Or was this about something else?

Breathe. Keep calm. Both things she'd perfected over the years in dealing with her father.

She'd spent almost twenty years waiting for her father to forgive her, for them to be a family again. She'd given up hope that having a family could ever come to pass. Unless... She would not subject her baby to the kind of life she'd lived, one filled with rejection and regret. But perhaps things would be different with Bobby. Perhaps *she* would be different.

If he said he loved her, she might say yes. If he talked of family, of more mornings like this—of growing old together—she might take the risk.

"Why?"

"Because you're pregnant."

The words cut to the quick.

She wanted to curl up and cry. She hated that feeling—of wanting something she would never get. Because that's what this had come to. She wanted something she had no right to want and she had gotten knocked down immediately for allowing herself that little fantasy.

At least he'd made his position known straight away. At least he had the decency to be honest with her, to not string her along. She had to respect that.

She owed him the same.

"No."

"What do you mean, *no?*"

She tried to push away from him—this entire conversation would be much easier if he weren't still clutching her to his warm, firm chest.

"I believe the word sufficiently explains my position, don't you?"

"We have to get married, Stella. This is nonnegotiable."

"Is it, now?" This time, she did manage to push herself away. "And why is that?"

"This is just as much my problem as it is yours. I'm trying to do the responsible thing here. I want to make this right." Every word was like a shard of glass cutting her skin. She'd briefly seen the possibility of a family. He only saw a problem. Then he went on, "Do you know what your father is going to do when he finds out? Do you have any idea?"

So that's what this was. He wasn't concerned about her. He wasn't even that concerned about the baby. He was, however, quite worried about his business deals with David Caine. It always came back to that. Always.

She scooted away from him and climbed out of the bed on the far side.

"Quite a good one, thank you very much. I've known him a tad longer than you have."

"No— Wait." Bobby scrambled across the bed after her. "That didn't come out right."

"It's fine. I understand completely. Neither of us asked for this and it's certainly going to mess up a great many of our plans." She ducked away from his outstretched hand, willing her voice not to crack. She would not cry. She was usually quite good at not crying. "I did not come here with the intention of marrying you."

Her voice cracked. Stupid, ridiculous hormones.

She circled around the bed and made a dignified, slow dash for the bathroom.

She'd known from the first moment she'd held the positive pregnancy test that she was on her own. She'd also known that raising this child on her own was inviting the wrath of her father in a way that made the past two decades look like a walk in the park.

But for a moment—a weak, glorious moment—she'd hoped that her father would have no place in this. That she would finally taste the love, the acceptance she so desperately wanted.

And then the moment had ended.

Bobby sat in the middle of his bed, staring at the bathroom door. What the hell?

He was *trying* to do the right thing here. Of course they needed to get married. That baby was his as much as it was hers, after all. They were in this together. And, yeah, a unified front would make dealing with the fallout a hell of a lot easier. Didn't she want him by her side when she told her father?

When he'd asked her to stay at his condo so they could work things out, he hadn't realized that would include her locking herself in the bathroom after she refused his marriage proposal.

Now what?

This was his fault. He'd rushed it. He was exhausted and not thinking clearly.

He'd thought the good sex—better than he remembered it—would prove his point. He hadn't been able to stop thinking of her for months—months where he hadn't even looked at another woman. No other woman could even come close to her witty charm, her edgy vulnerability. Stella was someone real. Someone who made him feel more real.

And now that he'd had her in his bed? Now that she was carrying his baby?

How the hell was he supposed to let her go?

He stared at the closed bathroom door. Okay, so the morning had blown up in his face. This was just one of those misunderstandings—a quick-but-honest apology, a well-thought-out explanation of his intent, and boom—problem solved. That's how it worked. No situation was so hopeless that communication couldn't make it better. He would know. Communication was what he did for a living.

Still…he needed to tread carefully here. Stella was unhappy with him. And the hell of it was, he wasn't exactly sure why.

Unless…unless she didn't actually want him the way he wanted her.

No. That wasn't possible. Women had never been shy about telling him that he was good-looking or that they appreciated how he made them feel. He could certainly afford to take care of Stella and the baby. So that couldn't be it.

Plus, she'd come all this way to see him. He had to mean *something* to her.

Okay, it was time to regroup. A tactical retreat was in order. He would give her a little space, apologize for his lousy sense of timing. And…

And then what?

Bobby shot out of bed and headed to the living room, the wheels turning in his mind. He still wanted a paternity test. Once he had results that proved him the father, then he could revisit the whole marriage thing.

He grabbed his laptop and typed *How soon can you do a paternity test?* into the search bar.

The first two suggestions would take several weeks, but the third option sounded like a winner. SNP Microarray—

a simple blood test that could be done at nine weeks, which was one week from now.

He checked his doctor's website, then called the number and made an appointment. The nurse said the earliest they could get the test done was in six days. The results would take another week. Maybe two.

Bobby took the appointment. What choice did he have? He could always send Stella home to New York for the test, but she'd said the flight was rough on her and he wanted to be with her. He wasn't sure why he felt so strongly about that—it was just a basic blood draw. But he should be there for her—both for the blood draw and for the results. That was part of making it right.

Which meant he was going to ask Stella to stay with him for another week, possibly two. Possibly three. For a moment, he allowed himself to think about how awesome that could be—fabulous morning sex, lots of cooking, really getting to *know* her. Figuring out what they were going to do next—that was sort of an important thing. He didn't want to send her back to New York without having a plan in place. Without a ring on her finger.

But—he'd rushed in like a fool. Would she tell him no again and have Mickey bundle her back East before the day was out? What if she cut him out completely? Could he bear to watch her walk away from him again—this time, with his child?

And that wasn't his only worry. He had obligations—legally binding obligations that would bankrupt him and his family if he failed to meet them. Like the obligation he'd already had to call Ben about. No way in hell he wanted to keep making those phone calls.

He had a reality show to film and a resort to build and a hell of a lot riding on the success of both. Sure, his brothers had invested heavily and he didn't want them to lose money over this, but it went beyond that. They'd already started the hiring process for the resort, although that would all be filmed for a later episode. It was no stretch to say that hundreds of people's livelihoods relied on the continued success of the show and the resort.

Hell, just last night, he'd been sitting in his trailer at the construction site, wondering how he was going to meet his deadlines. And that had been *before* Stella walked back into his life.

His mind spun. He heard a faint chime from the bedroom, followed by the soft sound of her voice. Probably that leprechaun calling her—checking up on him. Would she tell him that Bobby had seduced her with the promise of breakfast? Would she tell him he'd asked to marry her—and she'd said no? Would Mickey show up and shoot him in the knee?

If he asked Stella to stay with him until they received the test results, what on earth would she do? He couldn't let her anywhere near the construction site—too many cameras, too many eyewitnesses. Same thing with the Crazy Horse shop—if Cass, the receptionist, who took Bolton matters personally, got wind that Bobby had gotten a young lady pregnant, all hell would break loose. They hadn't had a family brawl since Ben had broken Bobby's jaw almost a year ago.

He rubbed his jaw where it had been wired shut. Yeah, the shop was out, at least until they had a plan.

If he was going to ask her to stay—especially after that disastrous marriage proposal—he needed to keep her happy. If he could figure out how she spent her days and offer her something close to that—she might agree to stay, to share the bed with him. She might even agree to reconsider his proposal.

He did what any self-respecting man grasping at straws would do—he looked her up on Google. He'd resisted the urge to do just that in the past two months. But now?

The first thing that came up was the link to her Twitter feed—but he noticed she hadn't posted much of anything in the past few weeks. Then a link to a Tumblr that seemed to be her posting pictures of style elements she liked. Not much to go on. But the third link was to an article in a fashion magazine: Stella Shines: A Model Designs Her Own Line.

It looked as if it had been a five-page spread—mostly photos, but with some snippets of an interview.

Wow. Stella was *stunning.* He'd known she'd done some modeling, but this? This was serious—and clearly, she was good at it. Her lithe body draped itself across his computer screen, her eyes seeming to look right into his. The clothes—all hers. He studied them—quickly, because he didn't know how much time he had before she emerged from the bedroom. Lots of black, but everything she wore was shot through with bright colors—even her hair had white-and-blue streaks in it. One dress was a flowy thing tied at the neck. The body of it was black, but it looked as if it had a kaleidoscope of color printed onto it.

"I started designing when I couldn't find anything I liked, romantic but with a jagged edge," the article quoted her as saying. "The things I found that claimed to be both weren't. It's as if grown women aren't allowed to be two things, hard and soft, at the same time. I want to change that. The only solution was to design what I wanted."

Bobby felt as if he should be taking notes. Buried in one of the comments was the information he needed. "I sew everything myself—but I don't think of it as couture. It's all bespoke. I'd love to open up a little boutique where women of all shapes and sizes can find a piece that suits them perfectly."

The article made scant mention of David Caine—just that Stella had attended the royal wedding with her father, the media mogul, in a dress that she'd sewn herself.

The article included a photo of father and daughter. Stella's dress was a deep navy with lace sleeves, a square neckline, a nipped-in waist and a flared skirt that came to just past her knees. Her hat was a thing that seemed to defy gravity with its long, sideways swoop that came to a point less than six inches from her father's chest. Although they were arm in arm, neither Caine was smiling.

He was wondering if that lace actually comprised tiny skulls, when she spoke from behind him. "Ah. I see you've found that shot."

Busted. He tried to chuckle and keep it light—as if she *hadn't* just refused to marry him. "It's the first time I've seen it. French toast?" Then he turned to look at her.

There was very little jagged about her this morning. She'd tamed her hair, but hadn't given it the precise edge it'd had last night.

But the bigger surprise was what she was wearing. Instead of one of her creations, she had on black lace leggings and an oversize cream-colored sweater that came almost to her knees. *Soft,* he thought, unable to stop himself as he slid an arm around her waist.

She fit against him as if she belonged there. He'd liked the feeling of her there from the very beginning, when he'd pulled her into his arms on the pretense of protecting her from a staggering drunk at the club. She'd felt so right then that he hadn't let her go.

Here she was again—a second chance at holding her.

He didn't know what she'd agree to. But while he had her here, he would savor her. So he leaned down and kissed the skin between the neckline of the sweater and her hair.

She made that purring noise again, but this time she pushed back.

"French toast would be lovely, thanks."

Her eyes were bright, though. She liked the attention. And she hadn't said no this time.

He took the hint. As he assembled the meal, she studied his computer. He wished he'd gotten it shut before she came out, but they were probably past the point of trying to hide things.

He cleared his throat. "I have an appointment with my doctor on Thursday. They can do a blood test—the paternity test—then. Just a simple blood draw." He walked over and shifted to the tab that had the test information.

"I see." She skimmed the page, tension holding her shoulders tight. She looked regal, despite the softness of her outfit. "Then what?"

"That's up to you." He'd showed his hand earlier. Now he had to play it cool. "I didn't mean to overwhelm you earlier. That wasn't my intent."

Her attention was still focused on the computer screen, but she cocked her head to one side and said, "Oh?"

"I wasn't thinking clearly—not enough sleep. I understand the situation isn't simple and you need to do what you think is best." He took a step closer to her and saw her back stiffen. "I'm sorry. It won't happen again."

She didn't do anything—not a wry comment, not a cold glare, not a warm touch.

Oh, hell. He'd always been able to talk his way into and out of any and every situation imaginable. That's what he did. That's who he was.

But around Stella? Not so much.

"Which part are you apologizing for—the sex or the proposal?"

There—he heard it. Buried deep under her indifferent tone was a witty observation. He hadn't lost her yet.

So he chuckled a little and said, "Why don't you tell me?"

She closed his computer but didn't turn around. Instead, she rested her hand on the tabletop. "Do you make it a habit of asking the women you sleep with to marry you?"

He leaned on the counter, keeping it casual. "Nope."

He saw the corner of her mouth crook up. "I don't want to get married."

Why not? And if not, why was she here? But he didn't

ask that. He didn't want to push her. "Understood. Will you stay with me until Thursday, when we can get tested?"

She nodded. Score one for him. "And then? While we wait for the results?"

"That's up to you. You could go home."

He saw her swallow as she dropped her gaze to somewhere near her toes. "Yes, I suppose I could."

But then, when the results came in, she'd be two time zones away. Just as he felt that he should be with her for the test, he knew he should be with her for the results. They were in this together.

"Or you could stay. As long as you like."

That was the right thing to say. He could tell by the way her cheeks pinked up and her lips curved into a small but distinct smile. She positively glowed. It was almost as if she was being lit from the inside out.

"What *are* we going to do with ourselves, then?"

First, they were going to have a lot more sex—good sex. The best sex he'd ever had. But what else could he offer to keep her here—and happy?

"Tell me what you do on an average day."

"Oh. Well." She took her plate from him and they moved to the table. "I work out, shower, sketch, sew. I'd love to have a little shop—a dedicated work space—but I haven't been able to get the financing yet. So I work out of my flat. That really covers it."

"Do you have clients? Orders?"

"A few clients that order on spec. I don't have a line yet. I'm working on it." She looked down. "My father covers my basic bills, so I don't have to work for money. But this is my dream."

"He won't give you the financing?"

"Ah, no." Her voice got quieter. "My business plan isn't a solid investment."

It wasn't? She obviously had the style and the talent to launch a line. Plus, with her name? Bobby wouldn't go so far as to say it would be a grand slam of an investment, but he made his living marketing. He knew a good idea when he saw one. And this seemed like a good idea.

"Why not?"

"I'm not responsible enough, apparently." He must have given her an odd look, because she added, "According to some people, anyway. I really don't go club hopping, you know, and I never pick up men. I only went to the party that night because I thought my father was going to be there and I hadn't seen him since the wedding."

"He *was* supposed to be there."

That seemed the easier thing to focus on, because Bobby was having a little trouble with the rest of what she'd just said. She didn't go to clubs? Didn't pick up men? He had no reason to doubt her—

But if she didn't do either of those things, why had she picked *him?*

Then, to his horror, he heard himself ask that very question. "Why me, then?"

She was studying her toast a little too carefully, slicing it into nearly equal bite-size pieces. "Do you know," she began, her voice almost childlike, "that people rarely talk to me?"

"I wouldn't have guessed that."

"It's true. To the vast majority of the world, I'm nothing more than David Caine's misfit daughter. They're all either terrified I'm going to be as cruel as he is or they want to suck up to me to get close to him."

He could almost see it—someone trying to charm her pants off in an attempt to get close to David Caine. Realizing that someone had done that made him want to punch that person. Hard.

"You didn't come off as a misfit in that article."

"Perhaps you should try telling my father that."

There was so much hurt in her voice that Bobby suddenly found himself more furious than he could remember being in a long, long time.

"He thinks you're a misfit?"

Not that Bobby had ever really liked David Caine—the man came off as a world-class jerk—but it was clear that Stella believed her own father hated her. Bruce Bolton, Bobby's dad, was a huge pain in his own right, but underneath all of that, he loved his boys.

"Oh, quite. He refused to take me to the wedding—said my dress was ridiculously inappropriate—but I threw such a fit." She smiled again, but it was a rueful thing, full of a deep pain. "Told him I'd already been cleared by security and if I didn't show up as planned, it would be suspicious and I was going and that was that."

"The lace on your dress—skulls, right?"

"Very perceptive. No one else noticed them." Her voice was little more than a whisper at this point. "I guess that's why—you *noticed* me."

He wanted to tell her it was impossible not to notice her—that compared to all the other women in that club, she'd seemed so real, so *true* to herself. How could he *not* have noticed her? But he knew if he said that, she might take it as something else—another fall-on-his-knees-and-propose kind of thing. And he knew she wasn't ready for that.

So he took her hand in his. He stared into her eyes, wide now with hurt and hope and worry. He could get lost in the depth of her eyes.

"Stella," he said, careful to keep his voice gentle, "I think it's time you tell me why you're here."

Seven

Stella sat there in a state of shock. What was he *doing,* for heaven's sake? Had he actually apologized for overwhelming her? Sincerely, even. He'd not only realized he'd upset her, but he wanted to make up for that. Was that possible?

Her father had hurt her so many times and never even noticed that he'd done so that she thought she'd become inured to the disappointment. He'd forgotten birthdays and Christmases for years with nary a peep of regret. She'd convinced herself that it didn't matter, that she didn't need those apologies.

That she didn't need to be noticed.

Bobby noticed her. Almost too much. Even now, he was expectantly waiting for her to pronounce what she wanted so that he could make it happen. It was such an odd thing, to be asked. Even Mickey didn't ask what she wanted. She stated her intentions—going to the club, tracking down Bobby—and he tried to talk her out of them before finally acquiescing to her wishes.

She hadn't known what to do with Bobby's apology a few moments ago—hadn't even known what the viable options were. She had even less of an idea what to do now.

What did she want? It was a simple question, really. But it wasn't. Nothing about this situation was simple. Bobby had said as much himself.

He was waiting on an answer.

"I want…" Stella bit off the words before they escaped

and betrayed her. She couldn't very well sit here and tell him she wanted a family less than half an hour after she'd flatly refused his—well, it hadn't been a proper proposal of marriage, but close enough. Even in her hormonal state, she was aware of how contradictory her thoughts were.

But a family was exactly what she wanted. Not a forced family, not one forged out of obligation or even desperation. One where all parties bound themselves together out of love.

Bobby patiently waited for her to continue, his gaze on her. He had such nice eyes—hazel green, flecked with gold that matched his blond hair. As further proof that she'd lost her fool head, she was suddenly possessed with the urge to sketch him.

She pushed back against the hormonal irrationality. She'd nearly said too much and now she needed to cover. A lifetime of practicing this skill with her father made it easy to do.

"I mean, I want you to be involved—calls, video chats, visits for birthdays and holidays. Perhaps when she's older, she can stay with you on break—that sort of thing." She couldn't meet his gaze any longer. She'd said this much. Might as well get it all out in the open. "She deserves a father. I want us to remain on friendly terms. For her sake."

She wanted so much more than that—but what was the point of pining for it? Bobby had offered to marry her. But she couldn't make him love her.

And she wasn't going to settle for anything less than that.

No, the sooner she stopped fantasizing about playing house, the better. What kind of marriage had he offered her? He'd give the baby his name, which would go a great ways in mollifying her father. David Caine would not tolerate a bastard sullying his good name.

But beyond that?

She waited, expecting Bobby to withdraw his hand,

lean back or even leave the table—to do something to put distance between them. Or, worse, ask what David Caine would want. Remind her of what her father would do when she told him. Or would he maneuver for the best position in his business affairs, now that he had leverage—her child?

Therefore, when he lifted her hand off the table and kissed her palm, she was so startled that she nearly fell clean off her chair.

"We're a little past friendly, don't you think?" he murmured, his lips still pressed against her hand. She felt the words more than heard them.

Her gaze flew back up. He was still watching her, that twinkle in his eye reminding her of how he'd looked at her when they'd met—as if she was the only woman in the room.

"Perhaps," she agreed, feeling mesmerized.

He grinned at her, but it wasn't something wolfish or predatory. He looked positively pleased—with her. That was such a foreign sensation that Stella briefly wondered again if she was dreaming.

Bobby shifted her hand so that it rested on his cheek. She was amazed at the prickle of his stubble against her hand. She was awake. Wonderfully awake. "I promise you that, at the bare minimum, I will call and write and video chat and visit on birthdays and holidays." He let go of her hand, but she chose not to remove it from his cheek. She didn't want to break this moment of connection.

Then he placed his hand over her stomach. "We Boltons are family men, Stella. We stick together. This baby will be a Bolton. I couldn't turn a blind eye to that if I wanted to—and there's no way my family would let me."

That last bit came out a bit differently, as if it were a great joke he was letting her in on. But was it? Was she giving him a choice? Or was this a sentence of community service in the name of family?

God, she didn't want him to be a good father out of obligation, no matter how amusing he might make it sound. She wanted him to want the baby—to want her.

With time, a voice whispered in the back of her head. Mickey's voice. *He'll come around with time. Just you wait and see, lass.*

Mickey had said those exact words to her about her father on numerous occasions. The first time had been the first Christmas after Mum's funeral. She hadn't seen her father for almost four months. She'd been sent off to the boarding school days after the funeral had ended. She was the youngest at the school by two full years, and the other girls had teased her mercilessly. When it was Mickey who arrived for her on the holiday break, the stony wall Stella had built up cracked open wide and she'd sobbed in the older man's arms.

Her father had not come for her. She'd spent months telling all those cruel girls that her father would fetch her because he loved her. Because he did not blame her for getting so sick in the middle of the night that Claire had run out to the chemist's and been hit by a drunk driver on her way home.

Because he wanted them to be a family again.

Mickey had driven Stella back to the cold, empty flat where she'd once been happy. A nanny had come to stay with her. Mickey had returned on Christmas morn with a small, poorly wrapped present for Stella—a doll with a red cloth heart sewn on its chest.

"He'll come around with time, lass," Mickey had promised as he rocked her on his lap. "I know your da. He still loves his little girl."

That was the problem with adults. They found it so very easy to lie.

Was Bobby lying now?

And if he was, did it really matter?

Maybe he saw the doubt on her face. It was as if he

could look past all of her walls and actually see what she was thinking.

"Once the results come in, we can contact a family lawyer—draw up an agreement. I'll need to arrange for child support and a visitation schedule. I'll support you however you want."

She nodded. Legally binding agreements, support and visitation—wasn't that what she'd just asked for? He was going to look after the baby. His voice was strong and sure. These were assurances, the very things she'd come all this way for.

So why did she feel so disappointed?

Bobby leaned forward, that charming smile doing its best to disarm her. Her body responded before she was aware it was happening. Even in all of her confusion, she remembered the way he'd looked such a short time ago as he held his body over hers—intense, hungry. As if he needed her. Almost as if he couldn't live without her.

That was it—that was what she wanted. Not that he would be there for the baby, but that he would be there for her. That he couldn't bear to have it any other way.

"If you change your mind and decide that you'd like to get married, my offer stands."

But Bobby didn't love her.

True, he didn't recoil in horror at the idea of marrying her, but he'd made his position clear. He would do it because that was what was expected of him. She couldn't bear the thought of binding herself to a man who didn't love her. She already had her father for that.

As much as she wanted Bobby, she couldn't let him hurt her. So she squared her shoulders and forced a pleasant, bland smile onto her face. The smile her father always took to mean that Stella agreed with him and the argument was over.

"Don't worry. I won't ask that of you."

Then she released her hold on him and turned back to her breakfast.

It had grown cold.

They ate in silence.

So much for his tactical retreat. But he couldn't seem to help himself when it came to Stella.

Bobby would have to stop trying to convince her to marry him, that was all. She had absolutely no interest in wedded bliss. Part of him wondered about the disconnect. How she could run so very, very hot in his arms—and then turn ice cold in a heartbeat?

He wanted her in a way he'd never wanted another woman. Yes, the sex was amazing and, yes, she was carrying what was most likely his child—but it went deeper than that. He liked that she was intelligent and beautiful and sensitive and soft and romantic with an extremely hard, jagged edge. He admired her ambition for starting her own boutique and her talent to actually pull it off—even if she hadn't lined up the financing yet.

She was the perfect counterpoint to his own ambition, but she didn't treat him and his success as something to be leveraged for her own advantage. Any other woman would have jumped at the chance to tie him down—to have a crack at the fortune he already had and the bigger fortune he was in the process of creating.

She didn't want him for what he had. That was a relief.

Sadly, though, it seemed as if she just didn't want him.

No. He refused to believe that—she *did* want him. He saw it in her eyes when she woke up. He felt it in her body when she melted against him. He knew it because she'd come all this way to tell him in person what a lawyer could have easily served in a lawyer's letter.

Which only left one other option.

She didn't *want* to want him.

And hell if he could make a bit of sense out of that.

They finished eating. He picked up the dishes and carried them to the sink. He liked to do the dishes. In some weird way, he thought better with his hands in a sink full of soapy water. That's where he'd had the idea for the destination resort and using a reality show to build his platform.

When she came to stand next to him, though, he tensed. She'd already refused him twice, but both times she'd come close to him afterward—which only added credence to his theory that she didn't want to want him.

"Thank you for making breakfast. It was delicious."

It'd been cold and the French toast had gotten soggy. Not exactly delicious in his book.

He shot her a sideways glance. Her head was down, which caused her hair to swing forward and partially hide her face. Despite that, he could feel her standing so close to him. If he wanted to—and he so wanted to—he could reach over, wrap his arm around her waist and pull her into him.

Which would probably be a bad thing, given that his hands were a sopping-wet mess.

"You're welcome."

He saw her turn her head in his direction. "I...I didn't picture you as a man who did his own dishes."

"I have someone who vacuums. But I like to do the dishes. I think better."

She nodded and fished a pan out of the rinse water. "I understand that."

"You do?" The fact that she hadn't looked at him as if he was nuts made it even harder to keep his hands in the dishwater.

But he wasn't going to touch her. Because if he touched her again, he might hold her. And if he held her, he might kiss her, and then make love to her again, which would make it that much harder to let her go when she went. Because she seemed hell-bent on going.

So he kept his hands in the dishwater as she said, "Oh, yes. Sometimes if it's late and I'm stuck on a design flaw and I cannot for the life of me figure out how to fix the problem, I'll put everything away, turn off the computer and go brush my teeth. And that's when I figure it out." She grinned at him—a small, private grin, as if admitting she brushed her teeth was almost as incriminating as him admitting he did the dishes. "But I have to shut everything down for it to work. If I leave my computer open..."

"No blinding flashes of inspiration?"

"Not a single one," she agreed in a sad-but-amused voice. "Then I have to decide if I'm going to sleep or get everything back out again. It's *such* a struggle."

He chuckled, but the whole time they talked, he was planning. She worked out, sketched, sewed. But Mickey had only carried in two bags. If Stella was going to stay, she would need something to do while he went to work. But he didn't have a sewing machine or whatever one used to make lace. And it wasn't as if he and Stella could hit the nearest crafts store for supplies, either. That would defeat the purpose of keeping her out of the public eye.

He was debating the value of asking Mickey to pick up some supplies, when it hit him—Gina and Patrice. They were the artists who lived in Ben's warehouse—they'd probably know where to get supplies *without* attracting media attention.

He and Stella could go over to Ben's place. The more he thought about this idea, the better it seemed. He could introduce Stella to his brother's family—show her that he was serious when he said Boltons were family men. They could borrow some art stuff from Gina and Patrice—enough to keep Stella happy while Bobby worked.

"So," she went on, her voice suddenly a little too bright. "What are you thinking?"

"I have an idea," he told her.

Eight

Stella clutched her bag in her hands as Bobby drove them through an industrial neighborhood. Parts of this looked like Manchester, England, and the gray tone to the afternoon was not helping. Not even the sky could manage to be cheerful.

Her nerves were getting the better of her. When Bobby had suggested that they visit his brother and pick up supplies from some artists he knew, she'd felt compelled to agree. He was trying to provide for her and she hated to disappoint him—even if that did mean she was going to meet his family.

All of those perfectly rational facts didn't quell the butterflies in her stomach, though. Neither did the huge warehouse Bobby parked next to. She hadn't prepared to meet his family. She hadn't prepared for any of this.

"Here we are," he said in an everyday kind of tone.

"Your brother lives in a warehouse?"

"Think more industrial loft. Wait and see." The twinkle was back in his eyes.

She did like that twinkle. It spread a pleasing warmth through her.

Bobby escorted her to an entrance, entered some numbers into a keypad and opened a gate. To a freight elevator? What in heaven's name?

"Industrial loft," he repeated, shutting the gate behind

them and entering another set of numbers. Then he stepped into her, slid his arms around her waist and said, "Hold on."

The lift lurched upward, taking her nervous stomach and pushing it over into upset. She clutched at Bobby, who seemed unaffected by the motion. "I've got you," he said, holding her steady.

"Better." She managed to get out as the nausea rolled her stomach. She really didn't want to meet part of his family and be sick all over their shoes.

Normally, motion sickness wouldn't even be an issue. But nothing about her was normal now. Being pregnant, being in South Dakota—being here with Bobby. Actually, given the total abnormality of the moment, she was probably lucky she was only a little ill.

She closed her eyes and buried her face in Bobby's chest as the lift came to an uneven stop.

"Hang on," he whispered as he pulled away. "Girls? We're here—but we're going up to Ben's!"

"Okay—not ready yet—meet you up there in a few!" came the excited response.

That was another thing that was not normal. After Bobby had proposed this little side trip, he'd had Stella make a list of supplies she would like—paper, fabric, tools—and called someone named Gina. This Gina apparently knew who Stella was—her voice had been so loud and excited that Stella could hear almost everything she said from several feet away. However, Gina had talked so fast that Stella hadn't been able to make out anything.

Bobby held her tightly and the lift began its unsteady climb again. She focused on taking long, even breaths, but her stomach was not happy.

Finally—mercifully—they stopped. With one arm still around her, Bobby opened the gate and ushered her out onto solid, unmoving ground. "You okay?"

"Morning sickness," she managed to get out through gritted teeth.

"It's three in the afternoon."

She'd love to sock him in the shoulder but that would mean opening her eyes and letting go of him, and she was afraid she might collapse if she did so. "I'm aware."

"Come on." He guided her forward. The sounds of Vivaldi filled the room.

"Hello," a pleasant female voice said. But her tone quickly changed. "Is everything okay?"

"Ginger ale? Or crackers?"

Stella couldn't tell if Bobby was asking her or asking the other woman.

"Yes," she said through gritted teeth. She willed her stomach to settle. Absolutely no getting ill and that was final.

Together, they walked through the industrial loft. When Stella got her eyes open, she was taken with the space—huge and very well done. The massive abstract paintings, which took up whole walls, should have made all the leather and mahogany furniture look out of place, but the space worked.

Bobby led her toward the kitchen area, where a stunning woman with a reddish-black braid that hung halfway down her back was sitting on a stool at a massive granite island. She glanced up as they approached, a weary smile on her face.

It was then that Stella saw what she was holding. A baby—not a newborn, but small enough to be tucked into a sling around the woman's shoulders. It had been ages since Stella had seen an actual child. Her friends, such as they were, didn't start families, and people with families didn't move in her design circles.

At the sight of the child something inside Stella clenched with such force that it almost doubled her over. That was what she wanted—a weary smile and a baby's red nose and what had undoubtedly been a long night of crying.

She wanted it all—she wanted to be the one person in the world that her baby needed and loved.

"Hello," the woman said. "I'm Josey—sorry about this," she added, waving her hand around. "Callie's been teething and has another double ear infection."

"Stella. No worries. Just some motion sickness. Wasn't ready for the lift. Nothing contagious."

Josey smiled and motioned to the glassful of pale amber soda at the far end of the counter. "I got that for you."

"Thanks much." Stella took a long sip. Refreshed, she took a step closer to Callie, who promptly began to fuss. "Oh, sorry."

"Don't worry about it. She's been clingy." This did not make Stella feel better. How was she supposed to be a good mum if babies didn't like her?

Bobby stepped around her, undeterred by the fussing. "More ear infections? Callie Lou Who, you can't keep doing that!" He reached out his arms and Stella was amazed so see the baby lean for him.

"I hate that nickname," Josey said, but she didn't seem bitter about it. Instead, she lifted the little girl out of the sling and handed her over to Bobby. Then she cricked her neck from side to side. "Thank you."

Bobby grinned as he chucked the baby under the chin. "You have got to let your poor mommy get some sleep, Callie Lou Who. Mommies need sleep, just like babies."

Stella stood there, dumbstruck as she watched Bobby cuddle the child. He was good with babies? He *liked* babies?

"Remember," he was telling the baby, who was almost smiling at him, "I'm Uncle Bobby—the fun uncle. Don't let Billy tell you otherwise."

That feeling—that clenching—seemed to center high in her chest. She was filled with a rush of emotions she couldn't grasp, much less name. Heavens, she couldn't even think of anything to say. She had no words for what she was watching.

"Been back to the doctor?" he asked Josey.

"He said if she gets two more ear infections in the next six months, we'll start talking tubes."

Bobby scoffed as he patted Callie's back. This is what she wanted so desperately. *This* was why she had come.

This is the family she wanted. The family no custody agreement could guarantee. These sorts of moments—that's what would be lost if Stella and the baby were in New York and Bobby were here in South Dakota. Sure, she knew Mickey would probably tote the infant around, maybe even sing her some of the old Irish folk songs from his childhood. But it wouldn't be like this. It wouldn't be her baby's father.

It wouldn't be Bobby.

He was grinning at the baby's mother. "So he likes to see you suffer—nice. Remind me not to use your pediatrician."

That snapped Josey's attention away from the baby, now nuzzled against her uncle's chest, back to Stella. Stella could see her connecting the dots—Bobby shows up with a strange woman, the strange woman requires ginger ale and crackers, then stares slack-jawed at the baby.

But Josey didn't say anything. Instead, she waited.

Bobby noticed the sudden attention shift. "Where's Ben?"

"Here," came the deep reply from the other side of the space. A tall, broad man who looked a great deal like Bobby was striding toward them, wiping his hand on a rag.

The two brothers—for there was no mistaking that—stood side by side. Ben Bolton was imposing and severe-looking in a way that reminded her of her father. Bobby was a few inches shorter and considerably lighter in his coloring.

Stella much preferred the younger brother to the older one. Ben seemed too harsh, too calculating—far too severe for her. But Bobby? He was warm and inviting and he made her smile.

In fact, the more time she spent with Bobby, the less she knew what to expect from him. Everything she'd thought she'd find—the self-made playboy, interested only in no-strings-attached sex and his next business deal—was offset by the unexpected. He gave up his bed so she could sleep alone. He made her breakfast and did the dishes. He brought her to meet his family and doted on his niece.

And he made her feel as if she was someone special. It was ludicrous to say that mattered, but it did. *Even though* she'd walked into his life and turned it upside down, he still looked at her as though he was glad she was there. As though he wanted something more from her. Almost— *almost*—as though he wanted her to stay.

Ben Bolton was giving Bobby one of those hard looks that Stella was all too familiar with. Then Stella realized that, instead of Bobby being resolutely blank or cowering in fear, he was actually grinning at his brother.

"You're scaring her, man," he said under his breath, but loud enough that everyone could hear it.

"Bobby was just introducing us," Josey added, but she didn't look as if she was trying to draw Ben's anger onto herself, as Claire had sometimes done for Stella. Instead, it seemed that Josey was just stating a fact.

"Right. Stella, this is my grumpy brother, Ben—the chief financial officer of Crazy Horse Choppers and one of the main backers of the resort. You've met his wife, Josey. She's a fundraiser for the Lakota Indian tribe and specializes in building schools."

Josey actually blushed. "*One* school. You always exaggerate." The way she said it was full of gentle teasing.

There was a pause. Stella stood as she always did when she was uncomfortable—shoulders back, chin up. She didn't betray any emotion that could be used against her.

"Ben, Josey, this is Stella Caine." Still holding the baby, he stepped to her and slid his hand around her waist. So comfortable. So easy. "She's a fashion designer and model.

We met two months ago at a party." He paused. "She's pregnant with my baby."

Well. No pussyfooting around *that*. But saying she was a designer first, a model second? Being David Caine's daughter wasn't worth mentioning? That summed up why she'd been attracted to Bobby in the first place. Because she was Stella Caine, first and foremost. David Caine had nothing to do with it.

She tightened her grip on Bobby as she leaned her head against his shoulder. *Together,* she thought. That was becoming a very good thing.

To be fair, neither Ben nor Josey blew their tops. Perhaps they already knew about the baby? Then Ben turned the meanest look she'd ever seen at his brother.

"Stella *Caine?*"

"Yes. David Caine's daughter." Finally, Bobby sounded as worried as Stella felt. She could tell this bit of information had caught Ben Bolton off guard. She could also tell that Ben Bolton being caught off guard was not a good thing.

"*The* David Caine? Who owns the show?" Josey asked, clearly flummoxed.

"Technically, he owns the network. He's only the executive producer of the show. I retained all rights during the contract negotiations."

This technicality did not make things better. Ben looked murderous, but Bobby was strategically holding Ben's daughter.

"We've got some testing scheduled for Thursday. Once we get those results, we'll see a family lawyer," Bobby added.

Josey seemed to pick up on Stella's distress. She got up and refilled the glass with more ginger ale. "Morning sickness—I've never heard a more misleading phrase in my life. I was always sickest around dinner." She poured herself a glass, too. "Why don't you give me Callie, and Stella and I will go chat?"

It was phrased as a question, but Stella heard the order loud and clear. Bobby was to hand over his infant shield immediately.

"Of course." Stella was amazed to see Callie had fallen asleep. "Oh, Gina and Patrice will be up in a bit. Stella's going to be staying with me while we get everything sorted out, and I thought the girls would be able to round up some supplies so that she can get some work done while I'm at the construction site." He cleared his throat. "For obvious reasons, we don't want Stella to be anywhere near a camera crew."

"Obviously," Ben snorted.

Bobby shot his brother a tense smile then kissed Stella on the cheek. "You'll be okay?"

"Will you?"

He kissed her again. "House rules—no fighting, or Josey gets mad."

"No one wants that." Stella couldn't help but notice Josey was looking at her husband when she said it. "The baby's asleep, boys. Let's keep it that way."

Nine

Bobby was not off the hook yet—not by a long shot. Just because Josey had laid down the law didn't mean that Ben wouldn't find a way to drive a knife deep into his back.

His brother stood there, arms crossed and eyes mean. So much for the hope that fatherhood would soften the uptight bastard a little bit. No such luck.

"I could use a drink," Bobby began, not so much because it was true—although it was—but more to get things started. If Ben had his way, he'd stand there glaring at Bobby until hell froze over. "Beer?"

"You're out of your damn mind," Ben growled as Bobby stepped around him—out of reach—and went to grab two longnecks.

Bobby got the distinct feeling that, as long as he didn't wake up the baby, Ben wouldn't kill him. He hoped, anyway.

"I didn't know who she was," he told Ben as he popped off the caps.

"Do you have any idea how much trouble you're in?"

"I didn't know who she *was*," Bobby repeated with more force. "We were on a first-name-only basis until after we…" He swallowed. "Until it was too late."

"You weren't thinking."

"The condom failed—I just didn't realize it at the time. This was an accident."

Ben snorted as he took a pull on his beer. "She tell you that?"

Bobby tensed midswig. "What are you saying?"

Ben let him sweat for several painfully long seconds. "You know what I'm saying. How do you know this whole thing isn't a setup? Do you even know if she's actually pregnant?"

Suddenly, Bobby wasn't so worried about Ben trying to punch him. Instead, he was far more worried about whether or not he'd wake up Callie by decking her father. "You watch your mouth about her. That's the mother of my child you're talking about. I'm just trying to make this right."

"What I said was to make sure it's yours—*then* make things right."

Bobby was hanging on to his temper by the skin of his teeth. "We have an appointment on Thursday." He said it through gritted teeth, but at least he wasn't shouting. "That was the soonest they could get us in. So you shut your damn mouth or I will shut it for you."

Ben didn't back down. He never did when he thought he was right. Which was all the time. "You've single-handedly managed to put this entire deal—*your* damn deal, I might remind you—at risk because you couldn't keep your damn pants zipped. Do you have any idea how much money *I've* put up for *your* resort?"

This was about money. Sooner or later, it always came back to that for Ben. He was a numbers guy. Sometimes, Bobby wondered what the hell Josey saw in him. Whatever it was, he couldn't see it.

"I know exactly how much you put in—twenty percent."

"Which is less than half of what David Caine put in, isn't it?"

Bobby didn't have an answer for that. The network was underwriting a big piece of the resort as part of the production fee. It was all part of the contract. The contract with all the morals clauses Bobby had broken.

Ben went on, his voice quiet but menacing. "Did you stop and think, huh? Do you *ever* stop and think? What if Caine decided he wanted out of the deal—but didn't want to pay the penalty? What if he put her up to this to get you out?"

"No," Bobby replied without hesitation, even as he wondered. "I don't believe that. She can't lie to me."

"Does that include not telling you who she was?"

Bobby glared at his older brother. It wasn't his place to tell Ben that the only reason she'd been at the party had been because she'd hoped to see her father for the first time in years. There was no way in hell that Bobby believed that Stella would do anything her father asked—including having sex in the back of a car. That wasn't her. He *knew* it. To think otherwise...no. It just wasn't possible.

"You watch your mouth," he repeated. "She says she's pregnant. She says I'm the father. I'm going to make sure that everything she says is true and then, when your wife and daughter aren't here, I'm going to come back and break your nose."

Ben had the nerve to almost smile at him. "That a threat?" He cracked the knuckles on his hands, one at a time.

Intimidation didn't work on him—he knew all the tricks, used them himself.

"That's a promise."

Ben changed tactics on him. Suddenly, his tone was almost apologetic. "Okay, say for the sake of argument that this is all just one giant, *amazing* coincidence. What are you going to do when Caine finds out you're screwing his daughter, huh?" Then, like a viper, he hit again. "Because you still can't keep your pants zipped, can you?"

Everything in Bobby's body wanted to come up with a denial—but he couldn't. There was a reason he was here— the same reason that Ben had been the one he'd called first. The only one he'd called. He needed his brother more than he'd ever needed him before. Ben was cool and logical and unrelenting. If he could get Ben on his side, he might have a shot in hell at figuring out what he was going to do.

Not that Ben was on his side yet.

"Yeah, thought so," his brother said. "That damn show you signed the whole family up for is going to disappear and take all of that funding with it and you and I and Billy are never going to see our money again. And if you think I'm pissed off, well," he said with a shrug, "you should think about what Billy's going to do to you when you tell him."

"I can fix this," Bobby said, his voice so quiet it was almost a whisper.

"How?"

"I asked her to marry me."

That set Ben back on his heels. "Really?"

"If we're married, then her father is a nonissue and the baby is a Bolton. Problems solved."

Ben seemed impressed with this plan—for twelve seconds. "And she said yes?"

She'd said no. Twice, no less.

There was no way Bobby would admit that to his brother, though. Just because Stella wasn't exactly jumping to get married didn't mean it wouldn't happen.

"We're going to wait on the test results." Not a lie. Just not the whole truth.

Ben snorted, but he didn't call Bobby out on this evasion. Bobby drained the rest of his beer as he looked toward the front of the loft. The damn place was so huge that he could barely make out Josey and Stella sitting on couches almost half a football field away.

"And then?"

And then…what? Then Stella would be three months pregnant and back in New York and he'd be in Sturgis, building a resort.

Unless he could persuade her that marrying him was what was best for both her and the baby.

Best for all of them.

"Then we get married."

He wished he'd managed to say that with a little more confidence. But it had come out...hesitant. Unsure.

Things Bobby hated.

"Look, let's just say that the deal *might* go south, okay? What do we need to do to keep the company safe?" This was Ben's specialty—the worst-case scenario.

Ben looked as if he wanted to hit Bobby. "Is that the royal we? You screw up, I have to fix it—that *we?*"

Bobby bit his tongue to keep from cursing. "I can fix this. But...just in case."

"You're a piece of work, you know that?" Ben gave him one of those looks that let Bobby know he wasn't fooling anyone, least of all his know-it-all older brother. "I'll run some numbers."

Ben turned to go, but Bobby grabbed him by the shoulder, knowing damn good and well he could get decked for it. "Wait."

Ben tensed, but didn't come up swinging. "What?"

"Just promise me this—don't scare her, okay? She's..." He struggled to come up with the right word. "She's vulnerable right now. I know Billy will scare the hell out of her and there's nothing I can do about that, but could you just *try* not to terrorize her? For me?"

Ben shot him a look that Bobby couldn't make out. It almost looked as if he approved. "Not for you," he said. "But Josey'll kill me otherwise."

Bobby took that. It was as good as it was going to get.

Stella followed Josey away from the two brothers. Everything felt wrong. Her stomach was wriggling around in nerves and nausea again. She sipped her ginger ale as Josey finally stopped at a seating area only ten feet from the lift.

"This is a lovely space," Stella said, wondering how to break the ice after that awkward introduction.

"Thanks—but you'll have to tell Gina and Patrice when they get here. They designed it." Josey stretched her neck, as if the slumbering baby was hurting her back.

Truthfully, Stella had no idea what to do with a child. But she was going to be a mum soon enough. There was no time like the present to start learning. "Would you like me to hold her?"

Josey regarded her for a moment. "That'd be wonderful," she finally admitted, looking tired. "Why don't you sit there," she said, motioning toward the leather sofa with the cushioned arms. "She needs to be upright—it keeps the pressure off her ears, so hold her like this." She nodded to the way Callie's face was tucked into her neck.

"All right." Stella sat and Josey handed over the baby. Callie was much heavier than she expected—heavy and warm and, now that Stella was holding her, she could hear how the baby girl whistled gently as she breathed. She felt perfect.

"There, you've got it."

"Right, then," Stella replied, afraid to move lest the baby flop away from her.

Josey took up residence on the closest sofa—close enough that, should something go awry, she could snatch the child out of Stella's arms. If Stella had any clue what she was doing, she'd be insulted. As it was, she was comforted by the proximity.

"So," Josey began with another measured look. "Tell me about yourself."

"Bobby covered all the basics—fashion designer, model, daughter of David Caine. What else would you like to know?"

Josey took a deep breath. "Look, I'm going to level with you. The Boltons are…an unusual group of men. They were raised to believe that family comes first—family is *every-*

thing. But within that unbreakable law, they fight like starving dogs." Josey glanced over her shoulder to where Ben and Bobby were standing in the distance. Stella followed her gaze. At the moment, they didn't appear to be fighting.

"Oh." She'd always had this vision of a family being perfect, gathered around the table in harmony. She could almost see a younger Bobby getting into scrapes, tussling with his brothers—but nothing that came close to starving dogs. The image scared her. "What will they do—as a family?"

Josey sighed, as if she'd had more than her fill of conflict. "More than likely, Bruce—that's their father—will order Bobby to marry you. Immediately. Billy will probably back him up."

"Oh."

Of course, Bobby had already offered marriage—and she'd said no.

There's no way my family would let me.

Bobby's words from that morning came back to her. He'd been joking—hadn't he? He'd made it sound light and humorous—but what if it hadn't been? What if he'd been serious?

Is that why he'd asked her? Because he knew that his family would force him to do it sooner or later?

Against her chest, Callie sighed in her sleep. God, how Stella wanted a family—but not one that was forced. Not because some angry men—men who weren't even *her* father, for heaven's sake—demanded it.

She wanted Bobby to *want* their family. She didn't want him to do anything so permanent as to marry her because he thought he had to.

"And your husband? What will he do?"

At this, Josey started chewing her lip. "He'll try to keep the peace. He always does. He doesn't always succeed, you understand."

"Of course." Not that she understood anything.

"So, before you get inducted into this family any more than you already are, why don't you tell me about yourself. And not the stuff that will come up on an internet search."

Stella let her eyes drift shut as she felt the little puffs of air the baby exhaled on her neck. This woman was on her side—she thought. If Stella could win over Josey, Josey might win over her husband, and that would even the odds against some frightful elder Bolton demanding a marriage for the sake of a baby.

Callie made a little mewing noise that made Stella's chest clench again. Soon enough—seven months, perhaps—Stella would be holding her own baby. Whatever happened here today—or didn't happen, such as it were—nothing was going to change that. She'd get her family one way or the other.

"My mum died when I was eight. I haven't seen my father in two years, not since he escorted me to the royal wedding—against his wishes."

A little color drained out of Josey's face. "Do you have any other family?"

"Only Mickey, my father's childhood friend. He's my security, I guess." He'd always been there for her, even when he didn't have any idea what he was doing. That had made her just secure enough.

"That's *it?*"

Stella nodded, trying not to hear the pity in Josey's voice. Her words dried up. For a moment, it felt as if all she could do was hold the baby a bit tighter. "I want my baby. I didn't plan on this, I didn't choose it, but I want my baby. More than *anything*."

"I see." Josey gave her a warm smile. It was exceptionally reassuring. "What decisions have you and Bobby come to?"

Stella swallowed. "He's been quite lovely about the whole thing. He's promised to call and write, visits for birthdays and holidays. Even agreed that later, when the child has a summer holiday, she could come stay with him. That's why he suggested the family lawyer—get it down in writing."

Josey appeared to think on that for a few moments, something like doubt on her face. "Is that what you want?"

Oh, this was painful. It had been bad enough having this conversation with Bobby—a man she barely knew but a man she was bound to, nonetheless. But she didn't know Josey at all.

Plus, this conversation was downright pleasant compared to how it would go with her father. Aside from Mickey, this was the friendliest audience Stella had. She needed to make the most of it.

"I want a family. I don't want my baby to be used as a bargaining chip in some sort of power struggle. I want her to know she is loved and wanted." Being loved and wanted herself? Well, she was used to disappointment.

"And Bobby?"

"Bobby." She looked back at the two brothers again. They were having a heated conversation, that much she could tell, but at least they were doing so quietly. "I don't want anyone making us get married, not if he doesn't want to."

"I see." Josey thought on that for a moment, but whatever else she might have said was interrupted by the clatter of the lift.

Just hearing that sound made Stella's stomach turn. She managed another sip of her ginger ale without waking up the baby. Perhaps she could do this, with practice.

"Oh, the girls." Josey shot her an apologetic look.

Before she could follow up on that worrisome sentiment, the gate opened. Out stepped two young women. The first woman had reddish hair, a tutu skirt and a skull-and-crossbones tee, all accented by a leather jacket and combat boots.

"We're here. Sorry we're late," she began as she hauled

out a huge storage tub. "Trying to find good fabric in this town is murder, I tell you!"

Then she saw Stella and froze, causing the second woman, wearing all black, who was also hefting a storage tub, to run straight into her.

"Babe," the second woman growled.

"Ohmygod—you really *are* Stella Caine," the redhead said in a rush.

"You know her?" Josey sounded bewildered.

"Are you kidding me? She's an *awesome* designer!" The redhead turned back to Stella, her words spilling out faster than coffee from an overturned cup. "You're an *awesome* designer! That dress you wore to the royal wedding? That was brilliant!"

"You saw the dress?"

"Saw it? It was perfect! Made that thing Victoria Beckam wore look like a sack."

"She was pregnant," Stella reminded her.

The redhead continued unabated. "I read you made the lace yourself?"

"I did." Stella suddenly felt shy. She'd never had anyone go quite so fangirl on her before.

"We've got a bet on that dress," the redhead said as the darker woman continued to gape. "Patrice said the lace was tiny skulls, but I said you wouldn't dare wear skulls to a royal wedding."

"Patrice, is it?" When the black-haired woman nodded, Stella went on. "Patrice was correct. Tiny skulls. No one noticed." Except her father. And Bobby.

"Pay up," Patrice said with a grin that could only be described as wicked.

"Later, babe," the redhead replied, seemingly not offended by losing the bet. In fact, she swatted Patrice on the backside before she pulled her into a hug.

Ah. They were a couple.

Josey stood. "Stella, this is Gina Cobbler and Patrice

Harmon, the artists who live on the second floor. They designed the apartment and did the art in here."

"We cook, too!" Gina added, looking proud of herself.

"The space is amazing," Stella said, wondering if she should stand and how she might do that without losing her grip on the baby.

"You like it? Ben let us do whatever we wanted. We helped Bobby with his apartment, too, but he had very specific ideas." Gina rolled her eyes. "No fun *at all*."

"I loved Bobby's flat—a real SoHo sensibility."

Both women looked pleased.

"So how long are you going to be in town?"

"A few weeks, perhaps." Then she made a gamble. "I appreciate you getting me some things to work with. If I find I need something else, can I call you? You could show me where the stores are."

"Really? That would be *so* cool! We should *totally* have a girls' day out!"

Then she looked up—they all did. Bobby and Ben Bolton had come forward.

"She really *is* Stella Caine! I totally thought you were pulling one over on us!"

"Good to see you, too, Gina. Patrice," Bobby added with a nod of his head. "How are you lovely ladies today?"

Now, *that* was charm. *Smooth* just poured off him. He shot her a wink—a small, hidden gesture just for her. He came to stand behind her, his hand resting on her shoulder.

Unconsciously, she clutched the baby a little tighter— too tight. She startled and began to fuss again. "Oh, sorry," she murmured as Josey swooped in.

"Don't worry about it—a little nap is better than no nap."

Stella supposed this was supposed to be comforting, but it wasn't. She was starting to feel claustrophobic. Too many strangers standing over her, wondering what kind of girl she was. Distrust was plain in Ben's eyes, less plain in Josey's, but still there. Stella was an outsider who didn't belong in this family. Even the odd pair of artists seemed better suited to this place than she did.

But, as they were all looking at her, she couldn't exactly slip away.

It was Gina who saved her. "Okay!" she said with a firm clap of her hands. "So here's what we got. The sewing machine is ours, but you may borrow it as long as you like—needle arts aren't really our thing." She pointed to a smaller case on wheels.

"We paint," Patrice said, gesturing with her chin to one of the huge wall-size canvases.

"Amazing," was all Stella could get out before Gina was off again.

"So there's the machine with the bobbins and stuff. Bobby said you needed yarn, but he didn't say if you wanted knitting or crochet."

"What did you get?" Bobby prodded her. He seemed at ease. Stella was actually envious. She hadn't been around this many people since, well, that night at the club.

Patrice popped open a tub. "Black, white, pink—six skeins of each, plus a set of knitting needles and a crochet needle to gauge." She pulled out a skein of white yarn. "Wool blend—is that okay?"

Stella ran her hands over the yarn. "This is lovely."

Patrice popped open the other tub. "Fabric."

"Oh, yes—the fabric! So we had a little fun with this—a lot of remainders, a little velvet—and some sequins!" Gina pulled out a truly garish piece of cloth, emerald green with sequins covering the lot of it.

The overhead light caught the whole thing, blinding her with the glow. "Oh, my."

Bobby gave her shoulder a squeeze. She reached up and squeezed back, wondering if she could telepathically communicate that she wanted to go home now. Or at least back to his place.

Bobby asked, "Did you get the sketch pad?"

"Oh—yes!" Gina rustled around in the first bin and produced two sketch pads. "Plus, graphite and watercolor pencils." She looked doubtfully at Stella. "I hope that's okay…"

"It's wonderful. Truly." Thanks to Gina and Patrice, she had enough raw materials to keep herself occupied whilst they waited for test results. Anything to keep her mind from dwelling on what would happen when they talked to her father and his.

"Great job, girls." There Bobby was again, being smooth.

"If there's something else, just call us! Girls' day out," Gina said, waggling her eyebrows.

"Will do." Suddenly, the feeling that had been claustrophobia turned sharply into sheer exhaustion. She had an irrational desire to have Callie's sleeping body nestled back in her arms so the two of them could doze away the afternoon together.

Soon, she promised herself. Soon she'd have her own baby, her own snuggles.

She managed to stand. Bobby's hand did not fall away from her. Instead, he stepped around the sofa and pulled her back into his arms. So easy. So comfortable. Without thinking, she rested her head on his shoulder. She couldn't ask for Callie back, but there was nothing to say she couldn't ask Bobby to take her home and lie down with her. She'd like to sleep in his arms, knowing he'd be there when she woke up. And then to feel his body against hers, in hers… Yes. That would be quite lovely.

Then she realized that everyone was watching them— his arm around her waist, her head on his shoulder. She and Bobby had done those things without thinking. Everyone else looked as if they were trying to read a fortune in tea leaves.

"Tired?" Bobby whispered, although she didn't doubt that everyone was straining to catch his every word.

"Yes."

"Can you handle the elevator back down or should we do the stairs? It's five flights."

The stairs? Good heavens, in her current state, she wasn't sure she could traverse that many steps without missing one. "We can try the lift."

"It was such a pleasure to meet you," Josey said, giving Stella an awkward side hug so as not to crush the baby. "Call me for anything. I'm home most days."

"Same here!" Gina offered with a perfectly polite handshake. "We can come to you, you can come to us—whatever works!"

Even Ben extended his hand. "It was a pleasure meeting you, Ms. Caine." He looked as if he was chewing on glass, but Stella appreciated that he managed to say it without growling at her. This must be him trying to keep the peace.

"The same. And your daughter is so beautiful." Ah, that worked. Ben's face softened. He could be handsome when he wasn't terrifying. Not the kind of handsome that set her body to singing—not handsome like Bobby—but still, she could appreciate the Bolton genetics.

Gina, Patrice and Bobby loaded the totes back into the lift while Stella traversed all the way back to the loo. By the time she got up front again, everyone was all smiles. She couldn't tell if they were faking it or not.

"Ginger ale for the ride home," Josey said, handing a to-go cup to Bobby. "Call me if you have questions about *anything.*" The way she said it made it clear that included not only pregnancy and babies, but Boltons, as well.

"Thanks so much." Stella entered the lift and sat down on one of the tubs.

Bobby stood behind her, bracing her with his legs. "The ride up was rough," he explained as the women shut the door.

"We'll go all the way down," Gina said as the lift lurched. "Just focus on breathing!"

"Will do."

Going down was much better than going up. Bobby rubbed her shoulders while she kept her head close to her knees.

Her mobile rang as they came to a lurching stop. She answered. "Hello, Mickey."

"Where are you at, lass? I thought the whole point of staying at his flat was that you would be *at his flat*."

Bobby opened the car door for her. "We'll get the stuff loaded—ask him to dinner."

She nodded. "Bobby took me to meet his brother's family. We're heading home now. Come round for dinner tonight."

"Took you to meet his own, did he?"

"He did. They're…interesting. He also had some friends get me sewing supplies so I could work."

"Is that so." It wasn't so much a question as a wonderment. Perhaps Bobby's actions were still too smooth, too charming, but at some point, sheer thoughtfulness had to outweigh that.

Because that's what Bobby was doing. Being thoughtful.

She checked the time. It was almost four and she needed to sleep for at least an hour. "Come to dinner and I'll tell you all about it." That was normal for them. They ate dinner together at least two nights a week. She'd tell him about her designs and he'd keep her up-to-date on what her father was doing. "Shall we say around seven?"

"Yeah, okay. You taking care of yourself, lass?"

She grinned. "About to go home and rest a bit. We'll see you at seven."

The trunk of the car shut as she ended the call, then Bobby slid back into the driver's seat. "Everything okay?"

"Just tired."

He started the car, but instead of pulling away, he leaned over. His fingers traced a path down her cheek. "You did an amazing job, beautiful."

"You think?"

"I don't think, I know. Come on," he added, finally putting the car into Drive. "Let's get you home."

Home. She was quite tired and hormonally messy, but it was the sweetest thing anyone had ever said to her.

Ten

Bobby was worried.

Stella had fallen asleep. He wanted to get her back to his apartment as fast as he could, but he was afraid to go even five miles over the speed limit. He found himself thinking murderous thoughts at people who were speeding or texting. If they hit him and anything happened to Stella...

So he putted along at a glacial speed, obeying all traffic laws and driving defensively. But his mind? That raced.

What if Ben was right? What if Caine already knew about this? What if he had been behind it? What if he wanted out of the deal? What if he was *using* Stella?

What if it was all a trap?

Bobby couldn't get his head around that. Ben's job was to work all the angles, run the worst-case scenario. He was good at it. He'd saved the company a few times because he'd been prepared for the worst.

But that wasn't Bobby's job. Whether his brothers liked it or not, he always saw the good in people. He figured out what they wanted and how he could give it to them.

Billy knew bikes. Ben knew numbers. But Bobby knew people. Even if there was some outside chance that he was being set up, he didn't believe it. He *couldn't* believe that Stella would allow herself to be used in such a way.

Besides, Ben hadn't been at the club. Bobby had. He had been the one to approach her, not the other way around.

So Ben was wrong about Stella and her motives and

Bobby was right. Great. This still left him with a hell of a problem—a problem that went far beyond David Caine and the deal with FreeFall TV.

He needed to marry Stella and she was in no particular hurry to marry him.

So she had agreed to stay with him for a few weeks. Sooner or later, Stella would walk away from him—again—because she thought it was best. He would probably lose his deal after David Caine got done dragging his name through the courts. He'd have no resort, a child who lived two time zones away and...

And he wouldn't have Stella.

He wouldn't have anything.

This wasn't like him. Why did he care so much whether she stayed or went?

He pulled into the parking garage and looked at Stella. Her chest rose and fell in even breaths, her mouth open just a bit. She looked completely vulnerable.

She hadn't taken him to her car because it would look good in the morning paper or because the exposure would grow her name recognition in fashion circles. He hadn't been a commodity to her. She'd chosen him because she liked him. Because he'd noticed her.

He hadn't known who she was. The more he thought about it...instead of working the room and finding the biggest name, he'd done something completely out of character. He'd spent the evening with a woman who had nothing to offer him.

Except herself.

Then it hit him. Yeah, he needed to marry her. The list of reasons was long. The baby needed to be a Bolton in both name and blood. It would make dealing with David Caine and that damn morals clause a hell of a lot easier. It might even save his resort—his dream.

All of those were rock-solid reasons he *needed* to marry her.

But he also *wanted* to marry her—to know for sure that she'd be in his bed every night, in his arms every morning. To know she'd be waiting for him at the end of the day so they could eat dinner together and talk. To see what she'd designed that day.

To see her nursing their baby, then rocking that baby to sleep.

Oh, hell.

He pushed those thoughts back—not because they scared him. Hell no, that wasn't it. Not even close. More like he'd gotten very little sleep last night. The whole situation was high stress. He needed to stop overthinking and focus on one thing at a time. The first priority was getting her to bed.

His pulse stirred at the thought. But Ben was right. He needed to keep his zipper zipped. Just because he'd broken the morals clause a couple of times didn't mean he could *keep* breaking it.

Unless she married him.

Which she didn't want to.

Which brought him right back to square one.

Okay, she was off-limits. He could exhibit a little self-restraint, no problem. He'd get her upstairs, tuck her in and do a little work before he cooked dinner.

But he didn't remember that plan including leaning over and pressing his lips against hers, or feeling her stir beneath him. And he was damn sure that he didn't plan on her sleepily looping her arms around his neck and humming into him.

He pulled away. He wasn't having sex in a car with her again. That was *final*.

"We're home," he said in a low tone as he stroked her cheek.

"Oh." She blinked at him, looking a whole lot more kissable. "Did I nod off?"

"Yeah. Let's get you upstairs."

He forced himself to remove her arms from his neck and open his car door. He unloaded the totes and the wheeled case with the sewing machine in it.

"I'll take that," she offered. As she said it, she stretched up, arms over her head, body long and lean.

The plan—he had to focus on that. He could think deep thoughts when he'd had more sleep or more beer—or both. Right now, he needed to get her upstairs. She probably wanted to go back to bed.

His mind immediately flipped over to the image of her tangled up in his sheets this morning, the camisole slipping down over her breasts, her body spread wide for his.

Desire shot through him. Even the way she wrapped her fingers around the handle of the sewing machine case sent a physical ache through him.

Maybe he should have let Ben punch him—anything to knock some sense into his stupid head. She was going to bed *alone.* As in, without him.

He grabbed the totes and hefted them to the elevator. Stella was already there, holding the door for him, seemingly unaware of how much Bobby was struggling to remain a gentleman.

For her comfort, he pulled her into a hug in the elevator. Only because he didn't want her to get unsettled the way she had last time. Yeah, right.

Working together, they got the two totes into the apartment. Once the door was shut, he said, "You still want to lie down?"

"A nap would be lovely," she said with a yawn. "Sorry," she added, her hand over her mouth.

Without another word, she walked back to the bedroom. It took almost every last ounce of willpower not to follow her down the hall. Instead, Bobby forced himself to make some coffee—extra strong—and turn on his laptop. He had to prove to Ben that he could make this right. And, most important, he had to keep his hands off her. She wasn't interested in anything but a friendly coparenting relationship. He needed to start honoring those wishes. Somehow.

He got a cup of coffee and sat down. Ben had that meeting on Monday with the bankers. This was an obligation that Bobby had to meet. And he'd signed that contract with the extensive morals clause. That was another obligation he had to honor. And he would. He was a businessman, damn it. A beautiful, pregnant woman sleeping thirty feet away didn't change that. He opened his file and started working.

"Bobby?"

At the sound of her voice, he froze. "Yes?"

He heard her clear her throat. "I thought you might, you know, join me for a nap."

Why was she torturing him? She'd already refused his proposal. Twice. How did she expect him to lie in bed and hold her and *not* make love to her—*not* ask her to stay with him for so much more than a few weeks? He couldn't hold her and not think about the way her body unleashed all that sexual energy on him—how she made him want to push harder, be *better*.

Couldn't she see that he was trying to honor her wishes—and the contract he'd signed? That he was trying to do the right thing here, for crying out loud?

He should not look at her, because if he looked into those pale, huge eyes—eyes hoping that he'd do exactly what he wanted and follow her back into the bedroom—well, he just might do it. And prove Ben right—he couldn't stop thinking about her.

So he did something that hurt. He closed his eyes and refused to turn his head in her direction. It was the only way he could trust himself not to take things further.

"I have to get these numbers crunched."

It was the cruelest thing he'd ever said and he knew it. She knew it, too. "Oh, right. Sorry to bother you."

The words—spoken slowly and quietly—sliced through

the air and into his back. It was nothing less than he deserved.

The next thing he knew, he was out of the chair and covering the distance between them in long strides. She'd lost the chunky sweater and stood in bare feet, leggings and a tank top. He was right—he shouldn't have looked at her, because there was no way he could resist her. He wasn't sure why he'd even tried.

She was in the process of turning away from him in disappointment, when he caught her in his arms.

"Oh!" she got out in a little gasp as he pulled her against his chest. He didn't even kiss her. He didn't have to. He just had to be there for her. That was all.

That was everything.

He half pushed, half lifted her in the direction of the bedroom.

"I have things to do," he told her, his voice rougher than he wanted it to be. "I have legal obligations that have to be met." Legal obligations he was actively breaking, just because he could *not* say no to her. "I can't let my family down."

But he was. He tried to tell himself it was because she needed him more than his brothers or the business did—but it wasn't the truth.

He needed her more than he needed the business.

"I know." She sounded confused—as if she'd expected him to say just that, but not while he was holding her. "I'm sorry."

"Don't apologize." They reached the bed. He pushed her down onto it, then stripped off his button-down shirt, removed his belt and kicked off his shoes. Maybe if he kept his T-shirt and pants on, he'd keep his zipper zipped. But that was a hell of a *maybe* and he knew it. "Tomorrow, I'll work and you'll sew. Deal?"

She sat on the edge of the bed, looking up at him with those beautiful eyes, as though she couldn't believe what she was hearing. "Deal," she finally said, a small smile curving up the corner of her mouth.

It wasn't that hard, was it? To give her what she wanted? Just a nap—an hour of sleep that he needed, anyway. He'd think clearer when he woke up.

She slid her feet under the comforter and scooted over, making room for him. He climbed in and pulled the covers up over both of them.

Stella was too far away. Damn it all, if he was going to skip work and lie down with her and run the risk of violating his morals clause *again* then he was going to hold her, by God.

Without asking, he slipped his arm under her shoulders and pulled her to him. "There," he said, settling his head back on *his* pillow—the one that now smelled of lavender. Of her. This whole situation—all of it—drove him crazy. Why did she have to be so beautiful, so impossibly sweet? Why did she have to make him want her so bad—and why couldn't he make her want him the same way?

"Happy?"

At first, she didn't bend then she nestled in his arm and placed her hand over his heart. "Yes. You?"

Everything was screwed up and for once he didn't seem to be able to talk his way out of it. But as he felt her body settle around his, felt her heartbeat against his chest...

"Yes," he told her as he laced his fingers with hers and held her tight.

And the hell of it was, he meant it.

The mobile rang.

Stella heard it on some level, but she was too comfortable to care. She couldn't remember feeling happier as she drifted in the space between awake and asleep. Bobby was here, his solid chest rising gently against her cheek, so she ignored the phone. The world could wait a little longer.

Her mobile rang again. This time, the ring tone sank in. She sat bolt upright in bed, dread curdling in her belly.

That was the tone for her father.

"Wha…" Bobby groaned as she leaned across his chest to snatch her mobile off the side table.

"Shh," she hissed. "Don't say a thing. Don't even breathe." She held the phone for one more second to compose herself and then clicked on. "Hello, Da."

"Where are you?"

That was her father's standard greeting and had been ever since she'd left England days after graduating from school.

"America. Where are you?"

That was also her standard reply. It was supposed to be snarky and ironic, but truthfully, she never knew where he was. Despite that time when she'd crossed the Atlantic without informing him, she'd been in the same place for almost seven years. New York City.

"New York." He sounded put out by this. "You weren't at your flat."

Stella swallowed, which only made the curdling fear in her stomach much worse. He'd come looking for her? She hadn't seen him in two years, for heaven's sake. Did this mean he knew about the baby? About Bobby?

Was he having her followed?

Her stomach turned hard, the dread so thick she could taste the bile in the back of her throat. She knew he'd find out sooner or later, but she had wanted to control the meeting—not be ambushed, not like this.

She pushed back against the panic. *No.* If he were having her tailed, he'd know where she was. Still, there could be nothing good about this call.

She was still half lying across Bobby's chest, his heartbeat calming. He started stroking her hair, which helped her keep her tenuous grip on composure. "True. I'm staying with a friend. Thanksgiving holiday and all that." So far, she had not spoken one word of a lie.

"Hmmph. And Mick? He's not picking up his mobile."

Good ol' Mickey. No doubt, he was sitting in his hotel room, staring at the phone and, more than likely, listening to the profanity-laced messages David Caine had left for him. But he hadn't picked up because he'd promised Stella that he wouldn't speak a word of the baby or of Bobby to her father.

"He's with me."

"He best be."

This surprising sentiment caught Stella off guard. It almost sounded as if her father was being…protective of her. Was that even possible?

No. It wasn't. She kept her voice light and airy. "You said you came round the flat?"

"Yes. I need you to accompany me to an event in two weeks."

"Heavens, and the last time I accompanied you to an event was such a smashing success. Don't you have a girlfriend you can take?"

The moment the words left her mouth, she knew she'd gone too far.

"I do not know how many times I have to tell you," David Caine growled. "There can never be another woman after your mother."

Guilt washed over her. He had, in fact, told her that very same thing many times before—so many times that she'd lost count. It should have been a comfort to her—her father had truly loved her mother. Perhaps he had not always known how to show it, but his devotion remained unwavering, even after all these years.

Indeed, it should have been a comfort. It wasn't. Every time, he reminded her that David Caine only had room in his heart for one woman—and at no time in the past, present or future would that woman *ever* be his own daughter.

"Sorry, Da."

"Now," he went on, his tone brusque, "I have been invited to a benefit gala in New York that's also a fashion show, or some such nonsense. You will accompany me."

"But you hate fashion. You won't even put up the seed money for my boutique."

"I don't give a rat's ass for fashion, and your store is a ridiculous idea," he snapped. "I can't think of a single person who would wear something you made. I've seen schoolchildren with more fashion sense than you."

Stella flinched. They'd had this particular line of conversation before, too—and she'd long since learned that listing the people who had requested a custom-order piece or noting the magazines that had featured her did no good. David Caine would never see her designs as anything other than a waste of time.

"This is good PR," he went on. "The benefit is for orphans or AIDS or something liberals bleed dry over. I've been taking a hit in Hollywood for my defense of traditional marriage. Some people think I'm heartless."

Stella couldn't help it. Her body curled into a small ball without her mind's permission. "Oh?"

Immediately, Bobby's hands rubbed her shoulders. Letting her know that he was still there.

"It's in two weeks. Wear whatever you bloody well want, as long as you're covered—I don't care. I can't have people thinking David Caine's daughter is a trollop."

Of course he didn't care. He couldn't care less about her designs, except when he thought they made him look bad. It had been much the same with her modeling.

Heartless. No one word could have ever described her father better.

"Two weeks?" She had things to do—test results to get, family lawyers to meet. He hadn't seen her in two years and he expected her to reschedule her life in two weeks?

She supposed she was to consider herself lucky that he had given her any warning at all.

"Tell him you'll check your schedule," Bobby whispered in a voice so soft she wasn't sure he'd said anything. But when she raised her head to look at him, he nodded in encouragement.

"I'll have to check my schedule. I'll let you know." There. She'd done it. A small victory.

"This is not optional, Stella. You will attend or—"

The way he said her name—as if it was a curse that couldn't be lifted—never failed to leave her feeling the way she'd felt in the cold, dank flat that first Christmas. Alone. Inconvenient.

Completely unloved.

"You will see what you can do," Bobby's voice was in her ear, so quiet there was no way her father could hear him. "Then hang up."

At first, she couldn't even form the words. Her father was probably trying to do her a favor by asking her to accompany him to a fashion event. She'd chat up movers and shakers and, if her dress was outrageous enough, perhaps wind up as a featured photo on fashion blogs. It would be a wonderful way to generate word-of-mouth buzz about her designs. It might even lead to an investor for her boutique.

But it wasn't optional. It was an order. David Caine went on as if he was the boss and she was the intern about to be escorted from the building.

That wasn't how it worked. Not anymore. He wasn't the one in control. She had a child on the way and that child had to come first—now and forever.

"I'll…I'll see what I can do."

"You *will*—"

Bobby took the mobile out of her hand and ended the call. They lay there for a moment in stunned silence. Bobby had just hung up on her father. She didn't know if she should be horrified or appreciative.

Then, against her every wish, Stella did something she had sworn that she would never do again because of her father.

She began to cry.

Eleven

Damn it all.

Bobby wrapped Stella's shaking body in his arms. He'd heard the whole conversation as clear as day. David Caine was not a subtle man in person *or* on the phone.

He'd only met the man twice—first to pitch him the show and second to sign the papers. Both times, David Caine had been belligerent to the point of demeaning, a real nose-to-the-grindstone Scrooge with a multimedia empire instead of a countinghouse.

That hadn't bothered Bobby at the time. He'd expected nothing less from high-level negotiations. The old man could bluster and threaten, but he couldn't browbeat Bobby into worse terms.

But for Caine to treat his own daughter that way? Damn. Bobby's father was a piece of work, but at least he cared for his kids.

Sobs racked Stella's body. God, it hurt to hear. He wanted to dent the man's skull in a few new and interesting places. No one should get away with talking to Stella like that, especially not her father.

If Bruce Bolton ever heard any of his boys talk to a woman like that… Men who treated women like doormats didn't deserve to keep breathing through their noses.

How dare Caine speak to his own daughter like that? This was exactly why they needed to see a lawyer before anyone said anything to that man.

Bobby curled his body around hers, trying to absorb her pain. He couldn't go beat the hell out of Caine, but he could be here for Stella. She clung to him. He didn't know what to say, which was unsettling. He always knew what to say, when to say it, who to say it to. But Stella always had him at a disadvantage. Something about her took everything he knew and threw it right out the window. So he didn't say anything. He just held her, rubbing her back and kissing her forehead, her cheeks.

Finally, she started to calm down. Sniffling, she forced the saddest grin he'd ever seen. "Sorry," she said, her voice all scratchy. "Must be the hormones."

"Don't apologize, Stella."

This statement made her tear up again, so he kissed her. Not the heated kiss from this morning, but something he hoped to let her know it was okay if she was vulnerable around him. He could be strong for her, if she'd let him.

A panicked series of knocks interrupted the kiss.

"Oh—Mickey—he's probably frantic."

They hurried out of bed. He put his hand around hers and they went to the door together.

Mickey actually looked about three steps past frantic. His face was red and he was panting. "Yer da," he said before he doubled over and coughed.

"I talked to him," Stella replied. But she didn't go to Mickey's side. She just clutched Bobby's hand a little harder.

"What did he want?" Mickey straightened up and took a good look at the two of them—her face all red, both of them still rumpled with sleep. "What were ye doing?"

Stella ignored the second question. "He told me I had to accompany him to a gala benefit and fashion show."

Bobby turned to look at her in wonder. Her eyes were still swollen, nose still runny, but she sounded as calm as he'd ever heard her. How many times had a scenario like this played out before?

Mickey's face twisted with confusion. "But—ain't that a bloody good thing? He's never cared a whit for your clothes. Ain't this him trying?"

"I—" Stella's voice caught and she covered her mouth with her free hand.

"Oh, now," Mickey said in a gruff voice as he fished out a worn kerchief from his back pocket. "Don't start with that."

Bobby watched the two of them. The whole exchange—they'd done this before.

It was clear from that conversation that David Caine had rarely, if ever, told Stella he was proud of her. Just that her designs—her passion—was childish. *Ridiculous.*

It pissed him off all over again.

His family didn't cry. They screamed and punched and threw things—but nothing was left unsaid. You always knew exactly where you stood with any Bolton. Bobby had often thought of it as a curse—years of fighting did wear on a man—but now he saw it for something else. A gift, almost.

His father never hesitated to tell him when he was being a jerk. But for every time Bruce said that, there were maybe two times when he slung his arm around Bobby's shoulders and said, "Good job, boy. Your mom would be so proud of you."

Yeah, Ben had torn him a new one over this whole situation. But he wouldn't grind Bobby's nose in this mess for the rest of his life. Something else would happen and they'd be back on the same side again, working to make the business successful. Bobby let go of Stella's hand and slid his arm back around her waist. He didn't know what was going on between them, what would happen once the baby came—but he knew he wanted them to be on the same side.

"The benefit is in two weeks," Bobby explained.

"So?"

"So we have some testing scheduled and an appointment with a family lawyer. That will take almost a month to complete."

Mickey didn't like that answer. His beady eyes narrowed. "Testing, eh?"

"We have to be sure before we tell my father. Otherwise…" Stella had recovered. Her voice, at least, was level.

She shivered, and he realized that she was only wearing the tank top and leggings. "You cold?"

She shrugged, but he felt the shiver race through her body. He had an idea. If she took a few minutes to powder her nose, he could get things straight with Mickey. "Grab my shirt, will you?" he asked as he gave her a gentle push toward the bedroom.

"All right." With a quick peck on his cheek, she headed back to the bedroom.

Mickey waited until the door clicked shut. "I ain't met the man yet who's worthy of her," he growled, one hand in his coat pocket.

Bobby knew he should be insulted—and he was—but he had more important things on his mind. "Are you going to shoot me or not? Because if you are, I'd appreciate it if you just got it over with."

Mickey glared. Perhaps the old leprechaun wasn't used to people calling his bluff. "No, I ain't gonna shoot you." He pulled out Bobby's gun and handed it to him. "She picked ye. It's not me place to tell her she's wrong. But I'm keeping yer bullets."

Bobby took the weapon and shoved it into a cabinet where Stella wouldn't see it. "Duly noted. Coffee?"

"Got any whiskey to go with it?"

"I can scrounge up something." He made the coffee. "I had some friends get her some supplies so she could keep working," Bobby said, motioning to the bins scattered around the apartment as the coffee brewed.

Mickey nodded in appreciation as Bobby handed him the spiked coffee. "Ye need to marry me girl."

"I can't."

"And why not? Ye could marry her on the side—keep it quiet. I don't want her having a bastard baby."

Bobby slammed his coffee mug on the counter so hard half the contents sloshed onto the floor. "You call my child that again and I'll break your jaw, gun or no."

"Easy," Mickey said—without even flinching, damn him. "Yer sharing her bed—more than sharing, I reckon. What's the problem?"

"The problem is that she already said no. Twice."

Mickey's mouth dropped open in shock. "She did *what?*"

"She has no interest in getting married and I'm not about to force her to do something she doesn't want. So no marriage."

"But—but—but the tests? Ye were gonna get tests?"

"So that no one can ever question the custody agreement." God, he hated this conversation. He was admitting to a near stranger that he'd failed. Yeah, he didn't want a bastard baby, either. But he would not force her hand. And he wouldn't let anyone else force her either. "She made her position clear. I don't want anyone twisting her arm because they think they know best—including you. You're not her father."

This statement looked as if it actually wounded the old man. "No, I'm not, but she's me girl just the same. Some families, you're born into 'em. And some you make."

Mickey's words hit him like a gut punch. He wanted to make this family work. Family came first. His parents had taught him that, lived it—family was everything. Family was the only thing.

He shouldn't want this family. He shouldn't be interested in tying himself to Stella until death did them part. He shouldn't even consider Mickey a father-in-law figure. He had no interest in settling down and giving up his lifestyle. He had parties to attend, celebrities to chat up, women to wow. That was his life—that was the life he'd planned on having for at least another five, ten years. If not more.

Behind them, the bedroom door opened. Stella emerged, looking put together. She'd brushed her hair, fixed her makeup and put her sweater dress back on. Still no shoes, he noted with an inner smile at her soft pink toenails.

"Behaving yourselves, gentlemen?" she asked as she handed over Bobby's shirt.

"Having a grand time, lass. Better?"

"Much," she replied as she kissed the older man on the cheek. Mickey patted her on the arm. Bobby saw the twinkle in his eyes, saw how Stella hung on his every word. They were gestures perfectly fitting for a daughter and father. Except that Mickey wasn't her father.

He shouldn't want her, shouldn't want to make a family with her. He *shouldn't*.

God help him, he did.

And he couldn't have one. He couldn't have *her*.

It would have been easier if Mickey had shot him.

Stella lay in Bobby's big bed, yawning. Dinner had been quite nice, actually. Mickey seemed to have warmed to Bobby a tad.

It was only ten-thirty and she'd had a nap, but she was struggling to stay awake. She'd always been something of a night owl, but this whole pregnancy thing was a different cup of tea. In fact, the only thing that kept her eyes open was the fact that Bobby should be coming in soon. He was showering in the other bath, to give her a modicum of privacy whilst she got ready for bed.

If she weren't so hormonal, the mere act of waiting for him would have her wired. She hadn't *slept* with a man in, well—ever. When she'd first come to New York, fresh out of school, she'd had a few something-to-prove one-night stands. Those men—boys, really—had never stayed. She'd *always* woken up alone, feeling hollow and used—a feeling made all the worse because she knew she'd done it to herself. No one had asked her to sleep around.

Eventually she'd realized that the sex was never worth the morning after. So she'd stopped. She'd only had two boyfriends who could have been considered semiserious. Even then, she hadn't let them sleep over at her place. She couldn't bear to wake up and find them gone.

She shouldn't be nervous about Bobby. After all, she was in his bed, his flat. Where was he going to go?

But she hadn't ever slept a whole night with a man. And that alone made her nervous. About everything.

For example, she was wearing a cami and a pair of knickers. That's what she always slept in. But was that the right thing? What would he be wearing? She hadn't actually seen him in the nude. She'd felt his muscles, had him inside her, but she couldn't say what he actually *looked* like.

For another, she wasn't sure where she was supposed to be. The bed was quite large—should she be on the far side? Where did he normally sleep?

She was going to stay awake for him, though. She wanted a whole night and a morning.

She wanted him.

You could marry him, said a small voice in the back of her mind that sounded a great deal like Mickey. *You could take him up on his offer. It might work.*

She closed her eyes and tried to envision the perfect life with Bobby. She'd have a shop with a playroom in the back so she could be close to the baby. Bobby would stop by on his way home from work and collect them. Then the three of them would go home and cook dinner together. After the baby was tucked in for the night, she and Bobby would curl into each other the way they had this morning. She would go to sleep knowing he'd wake her with a kiss and a touch that would lead to so much more. She wanted that more— wanted it every day. They could be wonderful together.

But it wouldn't last. Beyond the fact that her vision was

set in New York City, her world, and Bobby's world—his plans, his family—was here, she knew it wouldn't last. People didn't get happily-ever-afters, not in the real world. People died, fell out of love, cheated. Bobby would grow tired of the relationship, the effort—of her. She couldn't bear the rejection that was part and parcel of a divorce. She couldn't bear to have another man she cared about grow to hate her.

And she would not subject her child to that. Under any circumstances. No, she couldn't marry him. She had to protect herself. She had to protect her baby.

Her eyes were shut. She couldn't tell if she'd fallen asleep or just blinked for an extended period of time, but the next thing she knew, the clock said eleven-thirty—and she was still alone in the bed.

Something was off. How long did it take a man to get ready for bed? Surely not an entire hour.

She slid out of bed, not bothering to get the plush robe from the bathroom. The air was cool in the bedroom and the chill bit into her bare legs, shocking her awake.

She opened the door and listened. The flat was quiet, dark. Where was he?

She found her answer on the floor of the living room. Bobby was flat on his back, mouth open, snoring lightly underneath a blanket that looked much too thin.

Disappointment crashed through her. She'd so been looking forward to a night in his arms—and he'd chosen the floor.

She knew she should get back to bed before she woke him, but he startled. His eyes popped open. "Stella? Everything okay?"

"I was waiting for you."

"Oh, yeah. Sorry." He scrubbed a hand over his face as he yawned, seeming not sorry at all.

The rejection stung. She'd sort of understood when he'd first refused the afternoon nap—he did have things to do, things she was disrupting. But she'd assumed that he would come to bed tonight. Come to her. They'd agreed on it this morning, after he'd made love to her.

Hadn't they? Or had he just said what she wanted to hear?

"I thought you were going to sleep in your own bed." She swallowed, terrified of continuing, terrified of not. "With me."

Bobby froze for a moment and then let his hand fall away from his face. "But that's a problem, don't you see?"

No, she didn't. But she didn't want to hear how her need to be close to him was ridiculous. "Right, then. Sorry to have woken you."

She turned to go, but his hand on her ankle stopped her.

"Stella, what do you want?"

Such a simple question. Would she ever have a simple answer?

"I ask because your words tell me one thing but your actions tell me something else."

He still had a hold on her, his palm raising and lowering over her ankle and calf, warming her skin.

"What do you mean?"

"You know I've already broken my contract with FreeFall TV, right? By sleeping with you, getting you pregnant—your father could sue me for everything I'm worth and more, right?"

"Yes." She knew he wasn't trying to blame her for getting pregnant, but his statement hurt nonetheless.

"Just because I slipped up once—twice—doesn't give me permission to keep slipping up."

Of course. She understood now. That call from her father this afternoon had served to remind Bobby that her father held all the cards.

"The only thing that would negate the contract's clauses would be if we got married. Which is an idea," he added, sounding as if he was discussing the weather and not their lives, "you've already rejected. Twice."

It wasn't until that last word that she thought she heard something else in his tone—something that sounded hurt. But she wasn't sure.

You could marry him, that little voice with an Irish accent said in her head again. But was she really so desperate that she would agree to something as permanent as marriage just so she could feel, well, *loved?*

His hand was still running up and down her leg. "So tell me what you want. I feel like I'm doing a lousy job of guessing."

His eyes were still closed, but his touch—the warmth of the connection between them—had her kneeling next to him. His hand slid around her waist, sending heat through her body. What did she want?

"I want to go to sleep in your arms. I want to wake up there. I want you to make love to me. I don't want anyone or anything to say we shouldn't, we can't." She wished he'd open his eyes and look at her. But he didn't, so she touched his cheek. "I want to stay with you until we have the results. Just a few weeks. Can't we be together for a few weeks?"

A few weeks to pretend they were a happy family— happier than any she'd ever known. Surely he wouldn't get tired of her in that short time, would he? They could part as fond friends.

He put his other hand over hers, holding her palm to his cheek. He must have shaved after his shower. His skin was smooth.

"You're asking me to risk everything." For the first time, she heard something in his voice that she'd never heard before—fear. *"Everything."*

Wasn't that what she truly wanted—to be worth the risk?

"You did ask what I wanted."

His face crooked into a smile. "I did, didn't I?" Then his eyes opened, his beautiful eyes. There was no pain, no fear. He didn't look as if she'd burdened him with an impossible weight. If anything, he looked...satisfied. "You know what my brother Ben would say?"

She didn't know and she didn't care. She only cared what he would say. Would he send her away? Would he let her father and his damnable contracts rule him? Would he tell her that she couldn't have it both ways—it was all or nothing?

"What?"

Bobby sat up, pulling her into his chest. His strong arms folded around her as he pressed his smooth cheek to hers. Yes, this was what she wanted.

"He'd tell you that I *always* put the business at risk. I'm famous for thinking up the craziest thing in the world and then doing it."

She sagged against him in relief.

She felt the planes of his chest press against her breasts, felt the warmth of his body surround her.

"I suppose this is fairly crazy, isn't it?"

"The craziest. Hands down." Somehow, he got to his feet whilst cradling her in his arms the whole time. "Just for a few weeks, right?"

"Right." He carried her back to the bed and set her down. She slid over and held the blankets up for him and he climbed in after her.

Then she was back in his arms, back where she wanted to be. The only place where she felt she belonged. She could rest now.

"Stella."

She pushed back against the darkness of sleep. "Mmm?"

His arms tightened around her. "I'm glad you came."

He'd be there in the morning. She wouldn't wake up feeling hollow or tossed aside. For a little while more, at least, she could be content playing house with him.

"Me, too."

Then she slept.

Twelve

Stella had to pee. Badly.

This was not how she wanted to wake up with Bobby. True, she was in his arms—at some point, they'd rolled over and were now tucked together like spoons in a silverware drawer. It was lovely, really. If the pressure on her bladder weren't so intense, she'd lie here and enjoy everything about his front pressed against her back. There was a lot to enjoy.

But she couldn't. She had to go. *Now.*

Trying to move slowly so as not to wake him, she lifted one hand away. He didn't really need to be fully aware of her using the loo, did he? No, he did *not.*

With a *hmmph,* Bobby rolled free of her. It was something of a scramble, but Stella got out of the bed and into the bathroom with seconds to spare. She even got the door shut as she raced through it for a bonus.

Maybe he'd gone back to sleep. She'd been quiet, after all. Yes. She'd just slide back under the sheets and they'd pretend that nothing had happened. It was a good plan. She opened the door as silently as possible and stepped back into the bedroom.

Bobby was awake.

Well, perhaps awake was too strong a word. He was reclined on the pillows, scrubbing his cheeks with his hand but his eyes were open—and fixed on her.

He was *looking* at her. Intently.

"Good morning, beautiful."

"Ah, hello."

He leveled that devastating smile at her. "Second thoughts about what you said last night?"

She was envious of how cool he could sound about it, considering he'd just asked her if she'd changed her mind about sex. With him.

But the thing of it was, she hadn't.

"No. You?"

"Nope. But I kind of like it when you tell me exactly what you want. No confusion that way."

She took a step toward him. When she'd met him at that club, he'd made her feel fearless, unashamed to take what she wanted—which had been him.

"I want…" A smile curled one corner of his mouth. Even with the scruff, he was still far too handsome for her own good. "I want you to compliment me."

He didn't skip a beat, God bless him. "You are the most enchanting women I have ever met, Stella. An ethereal beauty."

She stopped and put her fingertips to her cheek, as if she was debating the merits of his statement—but mostly to disguise her grin. "And?"

He arched one sly eyebrow, making it clear that he knew they were playing a game—and that he approved.

"Your designs are brilliant. I'm constantly amazed at the work you create by hand."

She took another step toward the bed. "Is that so?"

He nodded enthusiastically. "I marvel at the things you can do with your hands. It's fascinating."

That made her giggle. "Do you, now?"

His sly look got much more intent. "I think about it *all* the time."

Feeling emboldened, she said, "I want to see you in the nude." She hadn't, really. He'd always been at least partially clothed.

A man should not look so sexy, she decided. It just wasn't fair.

"Would you like to undress me, or should I do it?"

Oops—she hadn't anticipated that question. Suddenly, she was nervous again. "I'll, um, watch."

Bobby was out of bed in a flash, standing just within arm's reach. First, he peeled off his tee, revealing a swath of skin and muscles that were so sculpted her breath caught in her throat. His chest was liberally sprinkled with golden-blond hairs that almost blended with his skin. She wanted to run her hands over his body. Several times.

Over one shoulder came a massive dragon's head. But it wasn't a black marking. The whole beast was rendered in vivid greens and golds, with streams of red fire breathing down onto the left side of his chest. It wasn't a hard, scary tattoo designed to instill fear—not like other biker tattoos she'd seen—but something else. Something artistic. Beautiful, even. He'd been hiding more than just muscles under his clothes.

Bobby hadn't noticed she was staring at the ink. "Like this?" He had the drawstring of his waistband in his hands and was undoing the tie.

"Yes, quite."

He managed to get the bottoms over a rather impressive erection. Stella was sure that the rest of him was now also bare, but she couldn't pull her gaze away from that one particular part.

He seemed quite…large. But perfectly balanced. Of course he was—everything about him was measured out in perfect symmetry, cut from the finest cloth. If she wasn't fully aware that they'd already had sex—really good sex—three times before, she might be nervous about being able to take all of him in. As it was, however, she felt her body tighten at the sight of him. Because that was for her—because she was enchanting and ethereal and brilliant and so good with her hands.

That was what she wanted—the feeling of desire building low and spreading through her body with a languorous heat. He turned her on, and she him. It was brilliant in its simple clarity.

If it had been her, standing there in her birthday suit for his inspection, she would have been nervous. Heavens, she was nervous and she still had on her knickers. But not Bobby. Instead, he worked through a variety of poses, trying to find the one that put his assets to the best advantage.

"Yes?" he asked, not even a little mortified by her humor.

"And you've never modeled," she said in awe.

"Nope." He struck a particularly garish pose. "Am I doing it wrong?"

Everything about him put her at ease. Well, everything except perhaps his jutting erection. That did other things to her. Her nipples—so much more sensitive these days—firmed up beneath her cami, which had the delightful effect of causing him to freeze, his gaze trained on her body. The need to have him went from languorous to heated.

But he didn't come to her. "What else do you want?" His voice was thick with strain and, as he lowered his arms to his sides, she saw him shake.

He was holding himself back, waiting for her to make the call. Amidst the desire that grew with each heartbeat, a second emotion gained a foothold. He was doing this for her. Because he cared about her.

"I want…" She stepped into him. His arms went around her waist. "No, not yet. I want to touch you."

"You are *killing* me, woman," he got out in a pained growl.

"Patience is a virtue," she replied as she let her hands move over him, starting at the wrists and working her way up his arms.

"Virtue may work for you, but not for me." But he lowered his arms. And shut his eyes.

She *tsked* him as she felt her way up to his shoulders and down his chest. His muscles were all but carved from stone—so hard beneath her hands. But she remembered how he'd felt when she'd curled into his body after her father's cutting words. A soft place when she'd needed one.

She didn't touch his erection as her hands skimmed over his thighs. He groaned, a noise of pain and frustration.

"Turn around," she ordered.

He complied, making the action sound as disgruntled as possible.

His back was a symphony of muscles, many of which twitched in appreciation as she touched him, storing his shape away in her memory as if she were measuring him for a new suit. The dragon took up most of his back, his front legs digging into Bobby's shoulder blade, his back legs pressed against Bobby's backbone and his tail curled low, right where Bobby's waistband would sit. She traced the dragon.

"Any particular meaning for this?"

His head hung. "Well, dragons are good luck."

"But?"

"My brothers told me it was stupid."

The detailing was exquisite. It had to have taken forever to complete. "So you did it to spite them?"

"No." Which he quickly amended with, "Not really. I've always had…big dreams. Crazy dreams. I wanted to own this town—this state. My dad never thought beyond the next bike, the next payday—but Mom…" His voice trailed off. "She told me all I needed was a little bit of luck."

"So you got a dragon."

"It's one of a kind. I destroyed the drawing after it was done. I wanted something no one else had."

"It's a work of art. Truly."

"Thanks." He sounded relieved, as if he might have been worried that she would agree with his brothers.

Her hands left the tattoo behind. When she got to his

buttocks, she did more than run her hands over them. She gripped them, feeling how his firm muscles filled her palms. He had an impeccably fine arse. She'd never done menswear, but for a backside that fine she might just have to try a pair of trousers.

"I'd love to measure you."

He groaned, a sound of pure agony. "You are going to be the death of me, Stella."

"Is that so?" Then, stepping into him so that her body pressed against his, she moved her hands around to his front and gripped his erection.

"Yes," he hissed out. But he kept his arms clamped at his sides.

With her face pressed between his shoulder blades, she slid her hands up and down his length. Yes, quite large. Warm and hard and quivering because of her touch.

As she stroked him—slowly—she breathed in his scent. The Gucci cologne was much fainter now. Instead, he smelled of clean linen, with a measure of something she could only call desire building underneath.

He filled her hands, low groans of pleasure reverberating in his chest. She did *that* to him. It made her feel exceptionally powerful, but suddenly it wasn't enough.

When she pulled away from him, he almost stumbled forward. "I want you to undress me."

She expected him to turn around, rip her clothes off and throw her onto the bed. She'd gotten him overwrought, after all.

But that wasn't what he did. Oh, he turned around, all right, and, cupping her face in his hands, he kissed her. The kiss packed a fair amount of heat—as did certain body parts that were pressed against her belly—but it wasn't something frenzied or out of control. It was the kiss of a man who knew exactly what he was doing.

He broke the kiss long enough to bend his head down to her neck. As his lips moved over her sensitive skin, he ran his fingers over the straps of her cami, then peeled them off her shoulders. As he worked the top down, he followed the fabric, pressing his mouth against her collarbone, then her chest, then her breast.

Heat flowed out from her center. Oh, yes. This was exactly what she wanted.

She'd told him to undress her, and that was what he was doing—but the way he was doing it? He'd known what she needed, even if she hadn't put it into words.

Desire had her trembling. It was the only thing she felt right now—no awkwardness, no nerves. It was completely natural that Bobby was now licking the tip of her right breast as his hands pulled the cami to her hips. It was also completely natural when he fell to his knees, pulling the cami and her panties off. Heavens, it was nothing but natural that he cupped her backside and kissed the top of her thigh.

She laced her fingers through his hair as he shoved her clothing down the rest of the way and let go of her long enough that she could step out of her things. He kissed her again. The length of his body pressed against hers, nothing between them—not even bedclothes. This time, there was more behind the kiss—more hunger, more need. His control was slipping.

She liked it—that he needed her so much that he couldn't hold himself back. He was giving her a kind of power over him.

"Tell me what you want."

That was the sound of complete surrender. She could do whatever she wished with him and he would accept it. Gladly.

She couldn't fight it any longer.

"On the bed."

The words were no sooner out of her mouth than he was back where he'd started, half reclining on the pillows. His erection stood at full mast.

She straddled him, feeling him rubbing against her. He leaned forward and caught her in another kiss as her hips ground down onto him. Every sensation she felt was focused on where he was touching her—his fingertips pressing against her hips, his tongue rasping over her lips, his erection straining to enter her.

She pushed against him, wanting him inside her.

"No, wait." He lifted her off, just far enough that he could lean over and grab a condom. It still seemed ridiculous—she was already pregnant, for crying out loud—but he'd already made his point about being tested.

As soon as he was sheathed, he pulled her back on top, settling her weight onto him. She shuddered with desire as her body willingly took him in. "Yes." Her voice came out more as a groan than an affirmation.

"Is this what you want?" he asked as he began thrusting, holding her hips steady—doing all the work for her.

"Yes," she groaned again, digging her fingers into his shoulders for balance.

"You're so beautiful, my Stella." As he said it, he kept moving, stroking into her with a wonderfully relentless pace. The heat built and built as he kept saying, "Mine," over and over.

His. That was what she wanted. To be his. And for him to be hers.

When he bit down on the space between her neck and her shoulder, though, she couldn't contain herself a moment longer. She would make him hers, if only for the short while they had together. She grabbed his hands from her hips and pinned them over his head as she rose and fell on him faster and faster.

"Stella," he said, trying to pull his hands out of her grip, but she held fast. "Wait."

But she didn't listen to him. She rode harder and harder, edging close to a climax.

"That's it, babe," Bobby said.

Her eyes snapped open and focused on his face. He met her gaze, his beautiful hazel eyes so deep she could get lost in them.

"Let me have it—let me have *all* of it."

Something in his words, his eyes— *Yes.* She cried out as the climax unleashed itself on her.

That had been exactly what she wanted. In the morning light, no alcohol to be seen—and he still made her feel this way. She loved him for that.

She was terribly afraid that she loved him.

Spent from the orgasm, she loosened her grip on his wrists. In a heartbeat, he had her by the waist again and was furiously pumping his hips into hers.

With a roar only muffled by his face against her neck, he came. The two of them collapsed onto each other, both panting from the effort.

He hauled her off him and disposed of the condom. Then they curled into each other as if they'd never been apart.

She traced a finger through the golden hairs on his chest. A kind of peace came over her, certainly helped by the excellent sex. She knew she could ask anything of him and, rather than have him shut her down, he would do everything in his power to answer.

"We'll chat and call and all that, won't we?"

"Of course," he replied, kissing the top of her head. One of his hands skimmed up and down her back.

"Even before the baby is born?"

"Even before."

"And you'll visit?"

"I'll be there for the delivery—assuming we have enough lead time."

That wasn't the answer she was looking for, however right it had been. "No, I mean—you'll visit, right?"

"Yes." But his tone of voice made it clear he hadn't quite caught her meaning.

"And when you visit, we'll..." She pressed her lips against his chest, right above his heart.

He didn't immediately reply, which made her feel as if she'd overstepped her bounds. She was presuming a romantic relationship that perhaps didn't exist—not outside this apartment for the next few weeks, anyway.

Then he ran his fingers through her hair, tilting her face up to meet his. "For as long as you want me, I'm yours, Stella."

Just like that, she knew two things. One, she was in love with Bobby.

And two, when she left him it would hurt worse than anything she'd ever experienced.

But she had to leave him. The sooner she made the break, the easier it would be to get over him. To stop loving him. The more she loved him, the more power she gave him—power to break her heart, power to break her baby's heart.

Yes, he would marry her—but not because he loved her. Because it was the proper thing to do—honorable, noble. The best of intentions.

But intentions didn't keep a woman warm at night. Intentions didn't give a baby a father who wanted her. Intentions weren't even promises.

Bobby could have the best intentions in the world, but that didn't change the fact that she could not bind herself to a man who did not want her as she was. To do so would lead to more heartbreak than simply walking away from him ever could. She couldn't risk her heart like that. She couldn't risk her child's.

She wouldn't let it happen, no matter how much it hurt.

So she said nothing. She merely kissed him while she still could. Soon enough, this would pass. All things did.

He didn't seem to notice the change in her mood. After he kissed her, he let her go.

"Now," he said, rolling out of bed. "We need to get to work."

"Yes." Needle, thread, cloth. If she was leaving, she might as well go to the fashion benefit. It was a good opportunity, after all. Yes, she would go.

Without him.

Thirteen

Sunday was one of the better days in Bobby's memory. He set his laptop up on one end of the dining room table while Stella set up the sewing machine on the other. She requested classic girl rock—the Bangles and Cyndi Lauper, that sort of thing—so they sang out loud as they worked. He made her laugh by knowing every word to Pat Benatar's songs, and she impressed him with her singing voice—clear and beautiful. Just the way she was.

The day passed quickly. She started knitting something, so she took up residence on the couch. Several times, Bobby caught himself staring at her. As far as he could tell, she wasn't using any pattern, but the yarn turned into lace before his eyes.

"This won't be true lace," she said when she caught him looking.

"Don't mind me. I'm just admiring what you can do with your hands." Her cheeks shot pink. "How did you learn to do that?"

"My mum," she said, and a happy smile lit up her face. "She taught me to crochet—that's with one needle, when I turned five, and to knit, that's what I'm doing now, when I turned six." Her voice was soft and light, her British accent stronger. "She told me that O'Flannery women—that was her maiden name—had been knitting for generations, passed down from mother to daughter. 'Twas my birthright."

The whole time she'd spoken, her fingers hadn't stopped moving. Bobby wondered if she could knit in her sleep.

Her face darkened and he remembered that she'd only been eight when her mother died. "Then, when I was at school, they took my needles away from me. I seem to recall I threatened to stab a girl with one for teasing me. But Sister Mary O'Hare took pity on me—as much as a nun takes pity, I suppose."

"Cracked your knuckles with a ruler?"

"Oh, yes. But Sister Mary took a shine to me and let me come up to her room and knit by the fire. The needles had to stay with her, but every night, I got an hour to work away from the other girls. An hour I could pretend my mum…" Her voice trailed off and Bobby thought she might cry.

Then everything about her shut down and she became unreadable.

"So you stayed the night at school?"

"I lived at St. Mary's in Cambridge full-time. Even though they didn't take boarders until thirteen, they made an exception for my father's money."

"You *lived* there?"

She nodded. "If he could, Mickey would come get me for Christmas break and take me back to our old flat. Then my father sold it, so Mickey and I, we started having Christmas at his flat." She managed a small smile. "A bit cramped, but very cozy."

Her voice was carefully level, but her fingers were moving faster than ever. *If* Mickey could—but not her father? What kind of man didn't make time to see his daughter on Christmas?

Not a good one, that's for damn sure. This had to be why she wanted "assurances" that he would call and visit for birthdays and holidays. He could not imagine anything sadder that a motherless little girl stuck at some heartless school run by heartless nuns, ignored by her father.

He finally managed to say, "Just you and Mickey, huh?" mostly because he couldn't think of anything else.

"Yes. Just me and Mickey."

It broke his heart—which was a new, painful experience. Aside from that one time when he thought he might be in love with Marla, he didn't get close enough to women to hurt for them.

But now? Listening to a woman detail a childhood of neglect while she produced knitted lace as if the whole world depended on it? He could just see her sitting at the feet of some severe nun, huddled by the fire for warmth, knitting as if the yarn was the only connection she had to her past. Because it was.

The feeling of his heart breaking changed and he felt furious. How dare David Caine cast off his daughter? He wanted to tell her that he would never turn his back on their baby. But everything about her was still closed off. It was clear she didn't want to talk about it—and he couldn't blame her.

"Is that for the benefit?"

Her face darkened, but only a little. Someone who didn't know her well wouldn't have noticed. But he did. "Yes."

"So you're going?"

"Yes."

So she'd decided. Which meant she would be leaving in less than two weeks. He was surprised at how little he liked that idea. He couldn't tell if that was because he would be waking up alone or because it felt as if she was bowing to her father's demands. Either way, he didn't want her to go.

Unfortunately, he was in no position to tell her to stay.

"Will you have it done in time to show me before you go?"

The corners of her mouth curved down, but a second later the look of sorrow was gone as she shook out the three inches of knit lace she'd produced while they talked. "I hope so."

That was all they said. The Go-Go's came on and they started to sing and work.

Even considering he took time to make lunch and dinner, he still got the numbers done that Ben needed. Stella had already gone to bed by that point. He wanted to climb into bed with her, feel her body curl around his. Such a small thing, but something he craved.

But he needed to do something, so he took advantage of the solitude and made a call.

"What?" Billy's voice was less than pleasant. In other words, he sounded normal.

"I need a favor."

"No."

Bobby ignored him. "I need you to do something cameraworthy on Thursday."

"What the hell for?"

"I have an appointment—no cameras allowed. I need you to be entertaining."

He could hear his oldest brother fuming through the phone. Billy did not like being a reality star, which was a crying shame because he was truly terrific on-screen. He cursed and threw things and glowered like a pro—all of which made for great television. They'd gotten the reality show because Billy had brought in a huge number of viewers to the webisodes that had come before the TV show. But part of the TV deal had been that Bruce and Bobby would be the focus of the show so Billy wouldn't get homicidal on-screen all the time.

Bobby waited. He didn't want to tell Billy about Stella—not yet, anyway. The big man had a surprising soft spot when it came to pregnant women and babies. If he knew about Stella, God only knew what he might do. Bobby was in no mood to find out.

"Who is she?"

Damn it all. Had Ben told him, or was he just that good at guessing?

"I'll explain later, okay? Just cover for me on Thursday."

Billy whistled. Bobby decided he liked it better when the big man was cursing at him. "You're gonna owe me for this, big-time."

"I'm aware."

"You doing the right thing?"

Bobby silently counted to ten. More and more, it sounded as if Ben had ratted him out. "I'm trying. Are you going to help me or not?"

"Yeah, yeah." And he hung up.

That went well. The only thing left to do was tell the production crew that they'd be at the shop on Thursday. He sent the necessary emails and shut everything down.

Then he went to bed, wrapping an arm around Stella's slumbering waist and listening to her breathe until he fell asleep.

He didn't want her to go.

But he didn't know how to make her stay.

They fell into an easy rhythm. He and Stella made all kinds of crazy love in the morning, then he went to work at the construction site, trying to make building a five-hundred-room resort as entertaining as possible. Most of the time, Mickey came over and did…whatever grumpy leprechauns did during the day while Stella worked on her dress.

The longer he was away each day, the more he wanted to go home—him, who'd been sleeping in this trailer rather than make the drive back to the condo for weeks on end. Things were different now.

He worked damn hard to be back in his condo by six so he could make dinner with Stella. She showed him her progress and he told her about the build. He couldn't quite see how her dress was going to come together, but there was no denying the handiwork that had gone into it.

At several points, he found himself looking at the

blueprints for his penthouse apartment. He had plenty of space—he needed to put in a room for the baby. Should he designate one of the guest rooms as Stella's? Or would she sleep in his bed?

The other thing he wondered about was Stella's shop. Her work was amazing, after all. He had space on the first floor of the resort blocked off for retail. What was stopping him from carving out a little of that space for Stella? She could have her shop with room to do the custom-made pieces she liked. The guests who could afford to stay at his resort could afford to buy a piece of her work, and her hard-yet-soft sensibility would fit right into the posh-biker theme.

Maybe, he reasoned, if he offered her a shop—the shop she'd been trying to get financing for, the shop she wanted so much—she would realize that he could give her what she wanted. That he could make her happy.

Nothing was stopping him from giving her some real estate…except Bobby couldn't bring himself to mention it. The chances were good she'd decline—politely, of course—because, really, her life was in New York and she'd already said no. He didn't want her to say no again. He didn't want to know there was nothing he could do to make her stay.

So he kept his mouth shut. He didn't talk about rooms or shops.

On Thursday, they went to the doctor's office. He held her hand while she had her blood drawn. He'd arranged for Gina and Patrice to pick up Stella after she was done—she didn't need to hang around a waiting room with sick people while he had his physical.

They had five business days to wait—next Thursday. Which was also the day Stella was flying back to New York, even though the benefit wasn't until Saturday. She said she needed a day or two for her stomach to settle, which seemed reasonable. But Bobby wasn't happy. He didn't want the doctor's office to call after she'd already gotten on a plane. He wanted to be with her.

What the hell was he going to do after Thursday? She would have regular doctor's appointments. It couldn't be that much longer before she'd be able to hear the baby's heartbeat. Was Bobby just going to let Mickey be the one to hear that heartbeat first?

No. He wanted to be there with her, *for* her.

But all she wanted was calls and visits, with sex when it was convenient. It wasn't a marriage.

It wasn't *having* her.

Somehow, he was going to have to live with it.

Tuesday was cold. So of course, that was the day the foreman wanted him out of the trailer to look things over. Bobby bundled up and stuck his hard hat on over a stocking cap.

As they walked the site, the camera crew trailing them, Bobby kept one eye on the sky. Maybe it would snow tomorrow and Stella would decide not to risk flying out the day after. And if she didn't make the benefit, then she could stay another week—for Thanksgiving. Hell, if the weather turned really nasty, she might be here until Christmas. And if she was here at Christmas, she might as well stay for New Year's.

Between these thoughts and the construction site, he totally missed the appearance of a long black sedan and the small man with red hair being escorted toward him by one of the contractors. Until suddenly a worried-looking Mickey was in front of him—and on camera. And by then, it was too late.

Dear God, he thought. *Stella. The baby.* "Is—" Then the camera guy moved for a better shot and Bobby remembered where he was.

"I need to 'ave a word with ye." Mickey didn't quite meet

his eyes, which made Bobby more nervous. "She's fine," he added under his breath.

"Sure, sure." Bobby turned to the camera crew. "Coffee break?"

The cameraman, who didn't have anything on his ears, nodded vigorously. Bobby headed toward the trailer with Mickey.

The moment they were out of earshot of anyone else, he demanded, "What's wrong? Is she okay? The baby?"

"All fine. Look, lad—I'm sorry about this, I really am."

Was the world's grumpiest leprechaun *apologizing?* To him? Damn—whatever it was would be bad.

"About what?"

"Davy's in yer trailer."

"Davy?"

Then it hit him. Davy—David. David *Caine.* Bobby stopped dead in his tracks, fighting the urge to grab Mickey by the lapels and shake him. "He's *here?*"

"He was worried about her." Mickey didn't manage to sound convinced by this statement.

"Like hell he was." More like Caine had threatened Mickey—although Bobby had no idea what would make Mickey betray his "girl." "You promised her."

Then he had a new thought. "Does he know she's pregnant?"

"I didn't tell him that." Mickey had the nerve to sound offended, which only made Bobby want to punch him.

"Does she know he's here?"

"No." He looked truly ashamed.

They were at the trailer door. Bobby gave the older man a forceful shove—something that normally might get him shot. He didn't care today. This wasn't about him anymore. This was about Stella.

"You better tell her—*now.*"

Mickey nodded, looking contrite. *Damn it all.* Bobby opened the door. He didn't know how he wanted to confront Caine about his treatment of his daughter, but he was pretty sure this wasn't it.

David Caine sat at Bobby's desk, looking over Bobby's plans as if he owned the joint. Which he sort of did, when you got down to it. He had a fifty percent stake. Without his money, Bobby had nothing.

He got the door shut against the wind. No one else was in the trailer—Mickey had probably cleared them all out. For the best, really—no audience meant no cameras.

Caine didn't look up when Bobby came in. He kept flipping through the blueprints, one page at a time—making Bobby wait.

He waited in silence. Caine obviously thought he was making Bobby sweat and Bobby knew that he had to give the man what he wanted. That was how negotiations worked—you gave away the small stuff and fought tooth and nail for the big stuff.

He was going to fight for Stella, by God. Tooth and nail.

So he managed to look uncomfortable and miserable as Caine ignored him, all the while praying that Mickey was warning Stella.

David Caine seemed…smaller than Bobby remembered him. Maybe it was the setting. The older man had loomed large in his posh office, seated behind a massive mahogany desk. In the cramped, dark interior of the construction trailer, he looked old.

Caine tapped a finger on the blueprints as if he was saving his spot and said, "Where is my daughter?" without looking up.

"At my apartment."

Caine took a deep breath, his stooped shoulders rising and falling with impatience. But he didn't look at Bobby. "And *why* is my daughter in your apartment?"

None of your damn business.

That's what he wanted to say. But he didn't—he couldn't. Not while there was a chance he could salvage his deal.

"She's my guest. She was going to stay for Thanksgiving but she decided to attend a benefit with you instead."

The only outward sign that Caine had heard him was a brisk tapping of his fingertip on the blueprint. "Impressive plans."

"Thank you." Which was met with more silence. It got to him and he offered up unnecessary information. "I want to live on-site, the better to make sure the resort is living up to its promise to guests at all times."

"I see."

Caine's attention was focused on the blueprints. "I also see," he said, his voice ominous, "that you've changed one of these rooms into a nursery."

Far too late, Bobby's eyes zeroed in on what was under Caine's finger—the Post-it Note he'd stuck onto the plans for his apartment that said *Baby's Room?*

"Yes."

"I didn't realize you were going to be a father."

Maybe Mickey hadn't told Caine anything. That didn't mean he hadn't figured it out. A man didn't get to where Caine was in this world without being smart.

"I am."

"You didn't say you were married when we negotiated the morals clauses of your contract."

Bobby swallowed. Breach of contract could end his show, his resort, all of his big dreams. It would be the kind of loss that a man never recovered from.

"I'm not."

One eyebrow—slightly bushy, but otherwise impeccably groomed—notched upward. "And who is the mother of this child?"

If Caine thought Bobby was going to give up Stella's name this early in the negotiations, he'd better think again.

"Someone I deeply care for."

That did it. Caine finally acknowledged his existence by raising his eyes. Bobby did not like the gleam of victory he saw in them. For one thing, it meant that Bobby was in very real danger of losing everything—*before* Caine had confirmed that it was his daughter who was pregnant. But it also told Bobby that Ben's first fear had been right—Caine wanted out.

"I'm sure my lawyers will have something to say about that."

Bobby stood his ground. He would not let this man bully him.

"I'm sure they will."

Just then, Bobby's phone rang. Stella's ringtone.

He knew what had happened. Mickey had called her, as promised. Now Stella was panicking. He wished he had an answer for her, but what did he know? Just that David Caine was here and he was not happy with either Bobby or Stella.

But was he here because of Stella or because he wanted a way out of his deal with Bobby?

Caine made a motion with his hand that was supposed to give Bobby permission to answer the call but looked more like a king deigning to notice a peasant.

Bobby could still salvage this deal. He had to believe that—to think otherwise was to admit defeat. Still, he wasn't sure how much longer he could tolerate Caine's attitude.

He pulled out his phone and answered it. "Hey."

"Is he there?" Stella sounded hysterical. Her fear went through Bobby like an arrow, one he wasn't sure he'd ever be able to pull out.

"Yes."

"What does he want?"

"I'm not sure. Listen," he added, trying to keep his voice as normal as possible, "I'm in the middle of a meeting. I'll call you back when I have a better idea on the time."

"Oh, God," she sobbed. Then the call ended.

Bobby stared at the photo of Stella he'd uploaded as her avatar—the shot from the club, cropped to her face. Her grin lit up the room. But it was just an illusion brought on by one night of lust and alcohol. The real Stella was damaged, broken into bits by the man sitting at Bobby's desk.

In that moment, Bobby hated David Caine. The feeling was so strong that it knocked him back a step. He didn't hate people—hell, he *loved* people. Every person had something good to give the world—or, at the very least, everyone had something to offer that made working with them worthwhile.

Or so he used to think.

And he had certainly thought that about David Caine. Caine had offered the means to Bobby's end—the show, the resort, the respectability. That's what Bobby had sold his soul—his family's soul—for. To be respected by his father and his brothers, to know that people thought of him as a serious businessman. That's why he'd signed the morals clauses. They were a legal announcement of respectability. That's why he'd done business with David Caine.

But now he was legally tied to a man who treated his family as well as he treated a disposable water bottle. A man whose mere presence left his daughter in a state of paralysis. Who ruled by fear, not by love. Not by respect.

But the deal… Bobby wasn't sure he was ready to kiss the resort goodbye just to tell David Caine where he could stick his morals clauses. The resort had not only been his deal, but his dream, his home. His future.

Except for Stella. Except for the baby. Weren't they his future now?

God, he didn't know what to do.

So when Caine said, "I'd like to see my daughter now," in the kind of voice that made it clear there would be no further negotiations, Bobby couldn't do anything but nod in agreement. The sooner they got this over with the better. At least, that's what he told himself.

When he got the door to the trailer open, he saw that Mickey had retreated to the sedan. Bobby mentally cursed the man, but at least he had the decency to look as if he was capable of human emotion.

Bobby waited for Caine. "You'll follow me back to my place?" As he said it, he shot daggers at Mickey.

"Yes," Caine answered, also staring at Mickey as he held the car door open.

"I called 'er," Mickey whispered as he walked past Bobby to the driver's door.

"I know."

"I'm sure sorry about this, lad."

"Prove it."

Then Mickey was out of earshot and Bobby was trying to do everything in his power not to run back to his car. He didn't know if Caine would tell Mickey to follow him or not. All he knew was that he had to get to his place first.

As he walked, he dialed Stella's number. Thankfully, his phone was connected to his car's speakers, so once he was in his car he could drive.

She picked up on the first ring. "Hello."

He sure as hell didn't want her sobbing, but the almost lifeless tone to her voice was even worse. "Stella, it's me. I'm in the car and your father is following me back to the apartment."

"Yes. I assumed that would happen."

"Are you okay, babe?" Because she didn't sound okay.

"Of course."

He took a corner a little too fast, causing the tires to squeal. The black sedan was hot on his heels, though. No losing Mickey. "What do you want to do?"

"To…do?"

"How do you want to handle this? He saw the blueprints for my apartment in the resort, where I'd added on a baby's room. He knows you're staying with me."

"You added a baby's room?"

Hadn't he told her that? Then he remembered—he'd

been waiting until after they got the test results. Still two days away.

"Yes. I was going to add a room for you. Maybe even space for a shop. We don't have much time, Stella—we'll be there in fifteen minutes. What are we going to tell your father?"

"I don't know, Bobby."

Her voice was soft now—and wavering. He changed his mind. He didn't want her to cry, not when she was alone and especially not when her father was about to show up for the first time in more than two years.

"Okay. Don't worry, babe. I'll be there in a few minutes. Whatever you want to do is what I want you to do, okay? If you want to tell him or not, that's your call. I'm not going to make the decision for you."

"All right."

"Stella, I—"

He wanted to tell her he loved her, but the urge was so sudden, so unexpected, that he fought it down.

"I'll be right there, babe."

The call ended. Bobby drove faster.

This would not end well. Someone was going to lose. He didn't know who or how much. The only thing he knew was that he'd fight for Stella.

Fourteen

Stella packed. She had a matter of moments before the quiet of Bobby's flat was shattered. She'd like to get through this with minimal screaming and even less guilt.

Her father knew where she was, that she'd been staying with a man—that alone was probably a deal breaker, as Bobby would say. She would not be allowed to remain, especially not once her father found out about the baby.

The baby who had her own room at Bobby's resort.

Maybe she'd heard him wrong. She was overwrought, after all. He'd never talked much about what would happen after she left. Sure, their time together had been lovely—easy, comfortable. The kind of life a woman could get used to. But it had all been short-term, pretend. She was going back to New York and Bobby was staying here. She'd made that clear because she couldn't risk the pain. He'd thank her for that, someday. His life was his family business and his resort. And her life…

Her life was her father's.

Although she hadn't seen him in two years, her life was still his. Mickey was his bodyguard, not hers—as evidenced by the fact that her father was in South Dakota. Her father's money paid the bills for her loft and for all of her design supplies. The only money she truly had was the small pin-money fund she'd earned from modeling.

So she packed. In went the lace dress she'd chosen to meet Bobby in, the sweater dress, the little camis she slept in. In went the nearly finished gown she'd sewn for the benefit, only five days away. In went her toiletries and her shoes.

In went her dreams for a happy family.

Now, now, she scolded herself as the thought made her throat close up. Her father couldn't take her baby away or send her off to a cold home for unwed mothers. This wasn't the nineteenth century. She was an adult now, not a scared little girl.

Then there was Bobby. Proof that he was the father was only days away. He had an obligation and had given every indication that he would honor it. Even if her father cut her off, Bobby would support their child. It wasn't as if she'd be cast out onto the street with no hopes and no prospects.

But she didn't know where that would leave her.

She shoved the unused yarn and fabric into a tote in the corner of the room and laid the small fascinator on top for Gina to give Patrice. It was made out of skull lace salvaged from her dress. Bobby would make sure it got to them.

Then she tried to make herself look presentable. Her father hated the way she dressed and did her hair, which was why she wore what she did. She was never sure if he'd noticed her unless he said something belittling. She got a decent edge on her bob and her makeup fixed as best she could. There wasn't much to be done about the puffy circles under her eyes. She knew she shouldn't have let herself cry, but she couldn't seem to keep her emotions in check these days.

Finally, she was as ready as possible. Her things were stacked neatly by the door. She stood in the center of the flat, taking calming breaths.

It wasn't more than a minute or two before Bobby burst in. She didn't say anything. She just wanted to look at him, to store the memory of his body, his face, with all the other memories. She needed to hold on to the way he'd made her feel.

He looked at her, then at her bags by the door, then back at her. "You're going to leave?"

The way he said it hit her harder than any slap in the face—as if she was betraying him.

She opened her mouth, but nothing came out. The next thing she knew, he'd crossed to her and, hands on her arms, kissed her in a way that could only be described as *savage*. It was as if his body was saying what he hadn't put into words— *Don't go. Stay.*

Say it, she thought as he held her. *Say it out loud. Give me a reason to stay.*

He didn't. Instead, he pulled back and said, "If you want to stay, I will fight for you." The light in his eyes was almost feverish.

Part of her wanted to swoon at the words. She wanted him, wanted to make a family out of the three of them— her, Bobby and the baby.

But she wanted him to want it, too. She didn't want him to bind himself to her out of obligation, and if David Caine was involved, obligation was all there was. Because Bobby hadn't said *I want you to stay.*

He'd said *if.*

From the hallway came the distinctive sound of her father grumbling at Mickey. Bobby turned to face the door. But he didn't release her, not all the way. Instead, one hand slid down and wrapped around hers. As impassive as she was trying to be, she couldn't help but give him a little squeeze.

They rounded into the doorway, her father first. He'd aged considerably since she'd seen him last. His hair had thinned and the lines around his mouth were deeper.

He was followed by Mickey, who looked like a dog that had been swatted with a newspaper. When he'd called, he sounded as if he'd been on the verge of crying. All he'd been able to tell her was that her father had flown in on his private jet, but Mickey hadn't told him she was with child.

Mickey met her gaze, then looked away. He did, in fact, look as if he might have shed a tear or two. She knew how it was. He'd tried his best to protect her, but no one refused David Caine.

Including her.

"Hello, Da."

There—she'd managed to keep her voice light and un-committed. That, in and of itself, was a victory.

"When I asked you where you were, I never imagined you'd be *here*."

No *hello,* no *how are you,* no *long time no see.*

Just like that, she felt small again, a little girl who knew, deep down, that she was nothing more than an inconvenience.

"Mickey was with me," she offered, knowing full well that wouldn't bring her any goodwill.

"Yes. I am aware."

Her father cast a disapproving glare around the room before his gaze settled on Bobby's hand holding Stella's. He stared, the tension in the room getting more and more painful. Stella felt as if she should say something, although she had no idea what, but Bobby gave her hand a sharp squeeze, so she kept her mouth buttoned tight.

Finally, her father said, "Why are you here?"

"I came for Thanksgiving."

It was true enough. By the time they'd gotten everything squared away with the doctors and the lawyers, it would have been Thanksgiving, except for the benefit.

"I was not aware that you knew each other."

"Well," her mouth started before she could process the words that were coming out, "I can't imagine why you would have been. I haven't seen you for two years. Rather hard to stay on top of these things."

Her father's glare cut through the air so fast that she could practically hear it. She should have been cowed, but there was something freeing in it. She would not want her baby to live in the shadow of fear of this man, as she did. There was no time like the present to begin living through example. She would *not* be scared of this man.

Which was well and good—until her father gave her the look that had always made her feel four inches tall.

"I'm only going to ask you one more time, *Stella*. Why are you here?"

She wanted so desperately to lie, to say something that would magically extricate her from this situation and turn the clock back to this morning, when Bobby had woken her up with a series of kisses that had gone places she'd never dreamed would feel so good.

Alas, no such lie existed. She took a deep breath and, Bobby's hand in hers, leaped into the abyss.

"I'm pregnant. Bobby's the father."

Behind her father, Mickey hung his head. He knew it, too—they'd gone past the point of no return.

Her father actually managed to look shocked. But it didn't last long. His face assembled itself into a mask of rage so pure, so vitriolic, that Stella suddenly wasn't sure they'd survive.

"Do you—" he spit out the words "—have any idea how that's going to make me look? After all the money I've given to support traditional marriage? Do you know what the papers are going to say? Good Lord, they'll crucify me—David Caine's daughter, pregnant out of wedlock!"

"Yes," Stella heard herself snap, "because this is all about your reputation, isn't it? Don't mind me. I'm just pregnant."

Bobby didn't say anything—really, what could he say? But he let go of her hand and slid his arm around her waist, pulling her into his hip. They still stood side by side, facing David Caine together. It didn't feel as if he was trying to hold her back. It felt as if he was supporting her, just as he'd promised. Just as *she* wanted.

"Don't you dare take that tone with me, young lady." He eyed them. "How soon can you get married?"

"We're not getting married."

Bobby's sudden interjection into the conversation made her jump.

"Don't be daft. You're getting married immediately, if not sooner. Otherwise—"

"Stella does not want to get married." Bobby's voice—clear and strong and, God bless him, not in the least bit intimidated—cut off her father midsentence. "So we're not."

The sentiment was lovely, really. Unfortunately, no one cut off her father. *Ever.*

Her father's eyes narrowed to murderous slits. "That's so, is it?"

"It is."

Bobby gave her a little squeeze. She loved him for it.

And he was going to pay for it, too. Her father would see to that.

"Did you take advantage of her? My daughter would never do something so stupid as sleep with the likes of *you*," he sneered. "I should have you arrested."

"I chose him, Da. He didn't take advantage of me. If anything, I took advantage of him."

Not that those words did anything to mollify her father. He was in a full-fledged rage and nothing would calm him down until he had taken his fury out on someone.

"My God, this is going to ruin me. Is that what you want?"

"No, I want—"

But he didn't listen. He never did. Instead, he turned his attention to Bobby.

"You listen to me, you little fink. You are going to marry my daughter or I will *destroy* you. I'll cancel your show, withdraw my funding for your real estate deal and make damn sure to publicize your gross negligence in every single newspaper, radio station and network I own. You'll not only lose that resort you're so fond of, but I won't stop until that god-awful motorbike business of yours is dead and gone." His voice moved past shouting and into a full roar. "No punk-ass rat makes a fool of *David Caine!*"

She'd heard those words many times over. No one ever made a fool of David Caine. It simply wasn't done.

The walls reverberated with the force of his scream. Then, a hush fell over the room. Her father seemed to shrink back into himself, as if the effort of his explosion had drained him.

He would do it, too—take everything Bobby had worked so hard for and grind it into dust. Not because that's what Stella wanted—she didn't—but because Bobby had to be taught a lesson, and that lesson was that David Caine always, *always* won.

Right then and there the words *Marry me, Bobby* were on the tip of her tongue. If that was what it took to keep her father from ruining the man she loved then perhaps that was what she needed to do. She couldn't bear to watch her father destroy the only man who'd come close to loving her.

But, as she opened her mouth, Bobby spoke.

"You watch your mouth around her."

It came out as a growl, as if he was prepared to launch himself at David Caine and fight to the death.

"I will not let anyone—not even you—speak to her like that. I don't care what you say. She's a grown woman and she has the right to make her own decisions. We're not getting married and that's *that.*"

Her father went positively puce with rage, but Bobby wasn't done yet, God bless him.

"You're not welcome here. If I see you anywhere in South Dakota, I'll file a restraining order. Now get out."

Had he just thrown her father out? Apparently he had. The shocked silence that settled over the room confirmed it.

But he hadn't let go of her. His hand was still around her waist. It was almost as if he wasn't *going* to let her go.

And David Caine saw it, too.

"Stella," he spat out as if her name were a bitter pill he couldn't swallow.

"You can stay," Bobby said. She turned to him, saw him swallow. His grip on her tightened. "If you want."

Not *don't go,* not *stay with me.*

She could stay. If she wanted.

Not because he wanted her to.

No, she would not cry and that was final. So she touched her hand to his cheek. "You'll hear from my lawyer," she managed to get out, although her voice was far too quiet to be authoritative. "About the child support and the visitation. Just as we discussed."

"Stella—" he said quickly, but stopped as she turned away from him.

She faced her father, who looked as if he might keel over. "All I ask is that you do not ruin him because of me."

She got no promises, which was just as well. She didn't expect any.

"My things," she motioned to Mickey, who looked as if he'd been run over by a train. "If you please."

Then, her head held as high as she could carry it, she walked past her father and out the door.

And away from Bobby.

Without crying.

Fifteen

Before he knew what had hit him, Bobby was alone in the middle of his apartment.

He was the guy who always knew what to say, when to say it—what people needed to hear. But he'd messed up, big-time, and he had no idea if he could make this right.

He hadn't wanted her to go. But he couldn't make her stay.

It was only two in the afternoon. He should go back to the construction site, pretend that none of this had ever happened. Those guys, the contractors and the hired workers, they all depended on the money from this build to get them through the winter. Some of them had turned down other guaranteed paying jobs to work on the resort. If Caine killed the whole thing—and Bobby put the odds of that happening on at least eighty percent—they'd all be out of a job.

And his brothers, Ben and Billy? They'd be out huge sums of money.

So many people had been counting on him. They'd all put their trust in him, believing that he could actually pull off this resort.

And Stella—she'd put her trust in him, too. She hadn't had to come out here and tell him she was pregnant. But she had.

He didn't remember driving to his brother Ben's warehouse. By the time his eyes focused, he realized he was sitting at his brother's table, his head in his hands.

"Bobby?"

At the sound of his name, he looked up—and found himself face-to-face with Jenny Bolton, Billy's wife.

"What's wrong?"

"Bobby's here?" At this, Josey emerged from the kitchen, Callie on her hip. "You're here!" Then she gasped. "What's wrong? Stella—the baby?"

"What baby?" Jenny asked.

There was no way around this, only through it. Better to tell Jenny and Josey first. Maybe, if they didn't hate him too much, they'd help soften the blow—blows—from his brothers.

"Stella and the baby are fine. But she left."

"*What* baby?" Jenny repeated with more insistence, her gaze darting back and forth between Bobby and Josey.

"What do you mean, she left?" Josey sat down at the table with a dull thud. "I don't understand."

"I don't understand, either."

"Someone better tell me what's going on," Jenny said, tapping her fingers on the table. "Now."

Bobby took a deep breath, but it wasn't deep enough to clear his mind. Maybe Jenny would understand. She ran a support group for pregnant teenagers. Even though neither he nor Stella were teens anymore, Jenny might have some perspective. Either that, or she was going to kill him. He had that coming, too.

"I got a girl pregnant. Woman, actually. She came to tell me and I convinced her to stay so we could figure out what to do. Then her father showed up."

Josey's eyes were wide with disbelief. "David Caine—he was *here?*"

"Wait," Jenny asked, looking impatient. "*The* David Caine—who bought your show?"

"Yes," he answered to both of them.

Josey covered her mouth with a hand. "How did he find out?"

"It's complicated."

"Try us," Jenny said, sounding grouchier by the moment.

"His childhood friend, Mickey, is Stella's bodyguard-slash-driver-slash-surrogate-father. He told David where she was. And David came to collect her."

He looked at Josey, hoping for something comforting. All he got were eyes wide with horror. "The show? The resort?"

All Bobby could do was shrug. "I don't know."

Jenny tapped one finger on the table with extra force. Bobby felt like he was a student who'd gotten in trouble at school.

"Okay, talk. From the beginning. Everything."

So Bobby talked. He started with the night he'd met Stella in the club and didn't stop until he got to the part where Stella left him. He didn't leave out a thing, including the part where he'd given the baby a room and hadn't told Stella about that. Not even the part where David Caine promised to ruin him.

When he was done, Josey and Jenny sat and stared at him. Callie had fallen asleep in Josey's arms, so she got up and put the baby to bed.

He and Jenny didn't say anything while Josey was gone. Bobby couldn't tell if that was a good thing or a bad thing. Jenny wasn't the kind of woman who kept her thoughts to herself. Shocked silence was not a good sign.

When Josey came back, she sat down next to Jenny, across the table from Bobby—like judges on the bench and he was awaiting his fate. Which he was.

He managed to clear his throat. "So."

"Man, you screwed *up*," Jenny said.

"I figured that out on my own."

"I have a question." Josey, ever the practical one, managed a warmish smile. "What do *you* want?"

"It's not about what I want, not anymore," he said, thinking of Stella's words.

Jenny and Josey gave each other a look Bobby recognized—the look they normally gave each other when one or more of the Bolton boys were doing something stupid.

"What?"

"Why are the cute ones always the idiots?" Jenny said to no one in particular.

"Bobby, honey, think about it." Josey spoke in the tone of voice she might use while trying to reason with a five-year-old about bedtime. "This whole thing has been about what you want—since the very first moment she showed up. That's all she's asked of you—to be honest about what *you* want."

Jenny was not quite as gentle with him. "You said she wanted a family?"

"Yeah."

Josey nodded. "She told me she didn't want to get married if *you* didn't want to."

He could see her confiding that to Josey. "So?"

"God, you're dense," Jenny muttered.

"Don't you have a kid to pick up from school or something?" Bobby snapped.

Jenny shot him a look. "I took the day off. I had an appointment." Then everything about her softened. "I'm three months along."

Great. And just when he thought things couldn't get any worse. Billy was going to be a father—and a good one. Bobby didn't have a doubt that Billy would be at doctor's visits, listening to heartbeats, holding his newborn baby.

The things that Bobby wouldn't get to do.

"Bobby, how did you ask her?" Josey was still being nice to him.

"What do you mean?"

Jenny rolled her eyes. "Did you drop down on one knee and tell her you couldn't live without her? That you loved her more than the sun, the moon and the stars above? Spout poetry? *Anything?*"

He thought back. He'd told her they'd get married. And when she'd said no, he'd added that, if she changed her mind, the offer stood.

"No…"

"For crying out loud," Jenny muttered.

Bobby gaped at Josey, who was nodding in agreement. "I'd bet dimes to dollars that she thinks you only proposed because you wanted to keep your show—not because you wanted *her*."

If the two of them were right… He dropped his head in his hands. All this time, he'd been thinking about the baby's room and the shop space, how much he wanted her to stay. He'd been thinking—*not* talking. Not with Stella. He'd been so hell-bent on asking her what she wanted that he hadn't told her what *he* wanted.

"I think he's got it now," Jenny said under her breath. She could have sounded smug but she mostly sounded sympathetic.

He didn't have anything—not Stella and…

"If I lose the resort, my brothers will kill me. They put their money into the resort—I'll cost them millions."

"Gosh," Jenny said in a louder tone, "I can't imagine Billy having ever done anything that was a poor business decision—like, say, paying blackmail money to an old girlfriend with a company paycheck."

"And I can't imagine Ben ever letting the company go down in flames when it conflicted with something he wanted—like, say, quitting because a certain brother canceled an equipment order," Josey added.

The two women looked at each other and grinned.

Bobby rubbed his jaw where it had been wired shut after Ben had punched him for canceling that order. "Yeah…I guess." But he was pretty sure that Billy would still kick his ass. God only knew how many bones would be broken this time.

"You're a creative guy. Even if Caine comes after you in

the press, who here gives a rat's behind?" Jenny was getting more animated now. "You'll spin it like you always do, use it to make you look more dangerous. What's the big deal?"

Were they really writing off David Caine's threats?

"But the money…"

Jenny shrugged, as if a couple of million in seed money were nothing. "News flash—money doesn't buy happiness. This David Caine—one of the richest guys on the planet, right?"

"Yeah…"

Jenny shot him a hard look. She could be a tough woman when she wanted to be, for a first-grade teacher.

"Is he a happy fellow? Is his daughter happy? Sounds like no. That's one thing I've never gotten about you, Bobby," she said, shaking her head. "You're incredibly well-off—the whole family is rich by normal-person standards—but it's not enough for you. What's all that money going to buy you?"

"Respect."

But even saying it out loud felt…wrong.

"Whose respect?" Jenny demanded. "Not mine. I respect actions."

"Not mine, either," Josey added. "And not Stella's. So what you've got to decide is, if you're doing this to get David Caine's respect, is it really worth it?"

Whose respect? He'd always told himself that he was doing all of this because he wanted to prove to his brothers that he wasn't the family screwup—a great game of one-upmanship. The resort was supposed to be his and his alone. Something he'd made with his own hands.

Except it had been a lie from the start. He'd *never* been able to go it alone. He'd had to get his family to agree to the show and kick in seed money. He'd had to rely on Caine's money. The resort might have been his idea, but it wasn't his alone. And when Caine got done with him, it never would be. By his own standards, he'd failed.

Except he'd had Stella. And the baby.

For a few happy weeks, Stella had made something with him that was *theirs*.

"They'll forgive you," Josey said into the silence.

Jenny snorted. "Eventually."

"Jenny," Josey hissed. "They'll forgive you, Bobby. I know they will. But will you forgive yourself?"

Her words cut him deep.

What had he done?

"I've got to go get my men," Jenny said. Her voice sounded far away, even though she appeared to still be sitting at the table. "Good luck, Bobby."

He couldn't even come up with words. Jenny left and Josey let him sit at the table, staring at the wood as if it held the answers.

His mind played over the past few weeks. He thought of the mornings—waking up with Stella's body wrapped around his, making love to her and then cooking breakfast for her. Of rushing home after work so he could make dinner with her. Of singing eighties pop songs while she knit and sewed.

Of how damn much he'd wanted her to stay for Thanksgiving. Of how he'd hoped for a blizzard so she'd be trapped in his apartment until Christmas and New Year's.

Of how she looked when he caught her patting her belly—still flat, but changing. Of how she'd looked with Callie in her arms. Of how he didn't want to miss being there when she heard the baby's heartbeat the first time.

Of how he hadn't been able to stop thinking of her since that night at the club, so much so that he hadn't even looked at another woman since then.

He was wrong—*so* wrong.

He had something he'd made right in front of him—a relationship with Stella. No one could take that away from him—not Caine, not Mickey, not his brothers.

He wasn't going to let Caine win. He'd never been deeper in negotiations, never had higher stakes.

It was time to make his move.

He had to go get Stella.

Sixteen

The Fashion for Humanity Gala and Benefit was crowded—
and secure. Wearing his tux, Bobby tried to slide through
the entrance behind a famous starlet in a backless gown, but
a bodyguard in a black suit got to him before he got inside.

"Name?"

At least Bobby was prepared. He'd crashed a few parties
in his day and knew the drill.

"Franklin," he said, giving the man a handshake and
slipping him a hundred-dollar bill.

The guy slid the money into his suit jacket and said,
"Name?"

"Come on, man." But he kept his voice bright and his
smile wide.

"No name, no entry."

To emphasize this point, the guard stepped aside for a
television star in a truly terrifying feathered gown. When
she was past, the goon squared around to Bobby, casually
flashing the piece under his jacket.

"Thanks for your time," Bobby said.

"Sure, buddy."

The guy moved on to his next victim as Bobby traced
his way back to the curb, careful to avoid the cameras that
were snapping shots of posing celebrities.

He hadn't seen Stella or Caine yet, but he wasn't worried. There was more than one way to crash a benefit.

It took a little walking, but Bobby managed to get around

to the back of the building. There, caterers in bow ties and white shirts were unloading vans of hors d'oeuvres. Bobby shed his jacket, waited for an opening and picked up a tray.

No one gave him a second look as he followed a waiter through the kitchen and into the reception space. He kept his eyes peeled for either Caine, but there were so many outrageous outfits that it made it challenging to see past the ruffles. No one had on lace.

Then Bobby saw David Caine, wearing an exquisitely cut tuxedo. He looked miserable as two men who appeared to be a couple tried to chat him up. For being at a Fashion for Humanity event, Caine appeared to be deeply uncomfortable with actual humans.

Bobby wanted to enjoy the sight of Caine squirming in the presence of a nontraditional couple. But he couldn't gloat from a distance. He scanned the party—no Stella. Where was she?

For the first time, Bobby considered that Stella had not come to the benefit, after all.

This put a crimp in his plans. Publicly professing his love to Stella with witnesses was hard to do when she wasn't present. For a moment he considered bailing, but he quickly changed his mind. He had things to say to Caine and he wanted witnesses—even if Stella wasn't among them.

He slipped off to the side to ditch the tray and his bow tie. He *was* at a fashion show—if he didn't have on a full tux, he needed to be making some other sort of statement. He undid the top three buttons on his shirt. That was as good as he could do.

The gay couple had been joined by a third man. Caine looked as if he was having dental work performed against his will. Bobby took a deep breath. No big deal—he was just going to create one hell of a scene. He grabbed a champagne flute and headed for his target.

"And Joel said—"

Bobby hated to cut the guy off, but he did, anyway. "Excuse me, gentlemen."

All four men turned their attention to Bobby. A rush of adrenaline hit him hard.

"You! What are you doing here?" Caine looked alarmed. He glanced around, as if he could summon a security guard out of thin air.

"Mr. Caine, I came to tell you that I reject your last offer."

"You *what?*"

Bobby cranked his neck to one side, then the other. His joints popped. The three gentlemen who'd been talking to Caine took a step back. The old Bolton moves were still the best.

"I'm going to marry your daughter, Mr. Caine. *Not* because you want me to, *not* because you're afraid that people will find out I got her pregnant and—this is the big one, Mr. Caine—*not* because you're going to cancel my show if I don't. I'm going to marry her because I love her."

"I—I—" Caine was sputtering. Good. Bobby had him off balance. "I don't know what you're talking about."

"Sure you do. You remember that I got your daughter Stella pregnant? You *do* remember your daughter, don't you? Or did you push her aside the moment she walked out of my apartment—like you always do?"

"I'm going to *destroy* you," Caine hissed, recovering from his initial shock faster than Bobby would have liked.

People were beginning to stare. He was all in.

"Like you destroyed your daughter? I don't get you, Caine. I'm sorry your wife died, I really am—but why do you hate your own daughter so damn much? What did she do to deserve it?"

Caine had turned an ugly shade of red and he'd lowered his arm so that what was left of his champagne was dribbling from the glass.

"I don't hate her. I'm merely disappointed in her choices. Like you, for example."

The three men all went "Ooooh" at the same time and a few others had begun to edge closer. Bobby could hear Caine's name being whispered around the room.

Bobby pitched his voice up a notch. "You treat your only daughter as if you wish you'd buried her with your wife."

Caine's color went from red to purple. He roared, "You *dare* talk to me like that?"

"You're damn right I dare. You don't own me and you don't own Stella. I'm going to do everything in my power to make sure that you never see your grandchild."

"You won't have a dime to your name by the time I'm done with you."

"I have something better than money, Caine—something you'll never have. I have a *family*."

With that, he turned around and walked out.

At least fifteen camera phones followed him. It wouldn't be long now.

Caine had promised to destroy him?

Two could play at that game.

Stella stared at her dress on the dress form. She didn't know why she was fussing over it. She wasn't wearing it to the benefit and her figure would change before she got another chance. It was a dress with no purpose.

But none of that stopped her from obsessing. Some part of her knew that she was distracting herself from reality, but she had no choice. Reality was something she couldn't alter.

"Maybe it's the rosettes?" she asked Mickey, who was taking his tea as he watched a football match on the telly.

"Couldn't tell you, lass," he replied without even looking.

Stella sighed. If Bobby were here, he'd get up, walk

around the dress and announce that, yes, perhaps it was the rosettes.

She winced in pain. Bobby wasn't here. That was that.

She'd been round and round this dress ever since she'd returned from South Dakota. She didn't like the lace—the pattern was too open. She'd planned on wearing nothing but a bra and some panties underneath it, just to give her father a heart attack, but the lace didn't cover enough. She'd tried the dress with a corset, but that hadn't been an improvement. So she'd sewn in a lining, only to rip it out.

Now she was fixated on the rosettes. The lace was floor-length and had long sleeves, thereby ensuring that she was completely covered, as her father had demanded. But she'd added satin rosettes to the neck and shoulder—huge fabric flowers that draped around the neckline like a cowl.

Perhaps that was the problem. Too many rosettes made it look dowdy. She'd take them off and add them back on, one by one, until she got it right.

What else did she have to do? At the very least, the dress would be a showcase piece.

She was snipping the threads off the rosettes when she heard a knock. A fairly insistent knock, followed by another round of knocking, even louder.

Mickey's gaze met Stella's. "Expecting someone, lass?"

"No," she replied, her stomach tightening. What if her father had come by? There was a chance he'd come to make amends. An incredibly small chance. Otherwise... "You?"

"No." Mickey hoisted himself out of his chair and went to his coat, where he extracted his revolver. "Stay clear, just in case."

Stella stepped down the hall and into the loo. If she peeked her head out, she'd have a clear view of the front door.

She heard the door open, heard a muffled male voice say, "I need to see her," heard Mickey reply, "Don't think that's the best idea, lad."

Bobby. Sweet merciful heavens. He was *here?*

Stella wanted to rush out to him and she also wanted to lock the door and pretend he hadn't come. The conflicting emotions had her stomach doing new and unusual things.

Why was he here? Perhaps he had the test results? Yes, that was it. She was too terrified to think of what else it could be.

"The hell it isn't, Mickey. Let me in. I need to see her."

"Give me one good reason."

There was a period of silence, which didn't bode well. What were they doing, having a staring contest?

Finally, she couldn't take it anymore. Bobby had come a great distance. The least she could do was face him.

She opened the door and stepped into the hall to find Mickey and Bobby standing in the doorway, both peering at…Bobby's mobile?

They looked up as she stepped into the room. Mickey's face was knotted up with confusion, the revolver forgotten at his side.

Bobby… Stella's chest clenched so sharply at the sight of him that she gasped. His eyes lit up at the sight of her—was it possible that he was happy to see her? That he'd missed her as much as she'd missed him?

Mickey sighed in resignation. "Keep yer cool and we'll all be just fine," he told Bobby, pocketing the gun. "But try anything funny…"

"I'm just here for Stella," he said, pushing past Mickey and walking toward her with long strides. In mere moments, he'd closed the distance between them.

She was no longer sure if she was breathing.

"What are you doing here?" she managed to get out in a surprisingly level voice.

"I came for you." He was close enough to touch, but he didn't reach out and grab hold of her as he'd done the last time he'd kissed her in his apartment.

Instead, he dropped to his knees.

"I screwed up, Stella. I've never screwed up so badly as I did the last time. I made you think that I cared more about the show or the resort—that I cared about what your father thought—more than I cared about *you*. That I *had* to marry you."

"Did you, now," she managed to get out, which helped her draw in enough air to keep from fainting.

"I don't have to marry you. My father can't make me and your father can't make me. Only one person can make me *want* to marry you."

"And who is that?" Was he possibly talking about Mickey?

"You. I want to marry you."

No. She would not cry. She squared her shoulders and tried to tamp down her emotions. "You promised to call and write and visit. I didn't ask you for anything else."

He shook his head. "You did. You asked me what I wanted. And I was so worried about what you wanted that I never answered the question." Then he held up his mobile. "You weren't at the benefit tonight."

She looked at it warily. "I was uninvited. And I couldn't get my dress to work. Did you go?"

She was certain he hadn't planned on attending. He couldn't get away—he was far too busy.

Which did not explain why he was on his knees in her flat on a Saturday night in half of a tuxedo.

"I crashed it." He grinned at her. "Had to go in the back with the waitstaff. That's where the rest of my tux is."

"I see." She didn't.

His grinned deepened. "You can't lie to me, Stella. I know you." He held the phone up again. "I wanted you to hear me say this, but you weren't there, so I had to hope that someone else would hear me say it for you." He tapped the screen and a supergrainy video began to play.

The title was *Is that David Caine getting shut down by a waiter?* It is! It was the middle of an argument, she gathered—and Bobby was clearly one of the men doing the arguing. The other was her father. He looked horrid. Which had been the whole reason she was supposed to have gone with him, to provide an insulating layer between him and the unsavory types who attended fashion shows.

She watched as they argued, watched as Bobby said, "I have something better than money, Caine—something you'll never have. I have a *family*." She watched as Bobby walked out of the frame. The clip ended.

"Saints help us all," Mickey muttered. "Davy's not gonna like that, not one bit."

Had Bobby really just thrown away his dream resort, his show? Had he really destroyed any hope of making peace with her father? Publicly humiliated David Caine—and had it caught on film? And for what?

For her. He'd done that for her.

Stella's knees gave.

Bobby sprang up and caught her halfway down. "Easy," he told her as they folded onto the floor together. "Can you get me a wet washcloth?" he yelled at Mickey.

Stella turned her face into his chest and tried to remember how to breathe. "Why did you do that?"

"Because this isn't about him." He brushed her hair away from her cheek and kissed her. *Oh.* Suddenly everything that had been wrong since her father had found her wasn't important.

"This is about you and me," he said when he pulled back from her. "I'm asking you to marry me, Stella—to be my family, to let me be yours. You have always been more important to me than any show, any resort ever could be."

A family. Hers. She had to close her eyes and lean against him again to keep the world from dancing to and fro. "You would give up all that for *me?*"

"Well," he said in that voice that Mickey had deemed too smooth. "I've still got a few tricks up my sleeve."

She met his eyes again. "What did you do?"

"You should know something about the Bolton brothers, Stella. When we put our minds to something, we're unstoppable." He said it with such conviction that a little tingle went through her. "I had to throw myself on their mercies, but Ben's lining up alternative funding for the resort. I'm thinking it needs to have a boutique in there—featuring clothes that are edgy but soft."

"Do you, now?"

He nodded. "It might take a while longer to complete. I'm going to have to pay for the lawyers out of my own pocket. The show is dead but that's okay. I don't need to be famous. I only need you."

He'd only mentioned the one brother. "Billy? Your father?"

"I told them I'd marry you because I wanted to, for no other reason." He hugged her tight, pausing only long enough to take a damp cloth from Mickey and press it to the back of her neck. "You asked me once what I wanted, and I never gave you a straight answer. That was my mistake, Stella—one I won't make again." He kissed her, his lips a promise. "I want to go to sleep with you in my arms and I want to wake up with you there. I want to make love to you for the rest of my days and I don't want anyone to say we can't. I don't want anyone but you. Just you. Just our family."

She'd promised herself she wouldn't cry anymore, but that didn't stop the tears. "Oh."

"So," he said with that cunning grin on his face, as if he knew he had her exactly where he wanted her. "What do you want?"

"I want a family." She'd told him that once, not daring to dream that it would mean all of those things he'd just said. "I want you."

His grin widened. "I like it when we want the same thing, don't you?"

"Yes, quite."

He kissed her again—harder this time. She let her fingers tangle in his hair, let her tongue trace his lips. He wanted her. To be wanted was a wonderful thing.

Mickey cleared his throat. "Right, then, you're going to marry me girl?"

Bobby looked at her and she nodded. "Yup," he said.

Mickey was insistent. "When?"

"Can you have a gown ready by Christmas?" he asked her. "You're not spending another holiday alone."

"That's rather short notice."

"I have full faith in what you can do with your hands. I think about it *all* the time."

She giggled and he caught her in another kiss. "Will you marry me, Stella Caine?" he asked in a quiet voice that wasn't meant for Mickey's ears.

"Yes," she said simply.

It was all she'd ever wanted.

Epilogue

As far as flower girls went, Callie left a little to be desired. Instead of throwing the flower petals from her tiny basket as Josey carried her through the doorway in the courtroom in City Hall, she turned the basket upside down and gnawed on the handle.

Then Billy and Jenny's son, Seth, came through the doors carrying the rings. They were still in the ring boxes—Bobby had not seen the point of a frilly white pillow for a civil ceremony. Thank heavens Stella had agreed.

The whole thing was surreal. Normally, on Christmas Eve, the Bolton men headed over to Dad's house. They ate steak and watched *A Christmas Story* and lifted a glass to Mom.

This year was different. Now, after a loud lunch at a nearby restaurant, Bobby was standing in a City Hall courtroom wearing a suit and a rose boutonniere. His brothers were lined up next to him. Even Billy had busted out a tie for the occasion.

The courtroom was relatively empty. On one side Jenny sat in front of Bobby's dad, Bruce Bolton, who was sitting with Cass, the receptionist.

On the other side sat Gina and Patrice, holding hands. Stella had decided against inviting anyone from her New York circles, although she had allowed Mickey to invite her father. He hadn't responded, which was just as well. Stella had wanted to keep this small and private and Bobby had agreed. Just family.

The doors opened again, and Bobby gasped. Stella walked in on Mickey's arm. She hadn't let Bobby see her outfit beforehand, essentially sewing the whole thing at Gina and Patrice's place.

"Worth it, isn't it?" Ben said over Bobby's shoulder.

"Yeah," was all he could get out.

Stella was wearing a pale, cream-colored skirt that went almost to the ground. Underneath, red peep-toe shoes peeked out with every step. For a top, she'd gone with a tuxedo-style jacket in the same cream fabric, the satin accents catching the light. She held three red roses in her hand—one for Bobby, one for her and one for the baby. The suit was close cut, hugging her curves. At three and a half months along, her curves were something to behold. To top it all off, she had on a small cream lace veil. Skull lace, of course.

It wasn't a traditional wedding dress, but then, this wasn't a traditional wedding. There were no other guests, no gifts, no lavish reception planned. Hell, they hadn't even gotten a minister. Just a judge who rode choppers on the weekends. The only camera was in Jenny's hand. No one else knew about the ceremony. This was private.

Mickey escorted Stella up to the front. Bobby was surprised to see tears in the old man's eyes.

Stella kissed the leprechaun before he gave her over to Bobby.

"You look beautiful," he told her, fighting the urge to pull her into his arms. There'd be time for that later.

The judge began to speak about them all being gathered here today, but he hadn't gotten far before the doors in the back of the courtroom opened up again.

Bobby's first thought was that the press had found out. After all, David Caine's daughter marrying the star of the reality show he'd recently canned would make for a juicy headline.

But then Ben's "Whoa" came at the same time as Billy's, "I'll be damned," which caused Stella and Bobby to turn.

There, in the back row, sat David Caine himself. He looked old and tired—but not angry. Which was saying something.

Stella's hand clamped down on Bobby's arm with a surprising amount of force. "Da," she whispered.

Bobby tilted his head in acknowledgment of the older man before he turned to his bride. "I knew he'd come around."

Stella's eyes glittered with happy tears. "He did, did he?"

Bobby nodded, wrapping his fingers around hers. "I think he's starting to realize that family is everything." Then he leaned in. "*You're* my everything, Stella."

Then the judge cleared his throat and made it official.

She was his everything.

She always would be.

* * * * *

If you liked Bobby's story,
don't miss any of THE BOLTON BROTHERS *trilogy*
by Sarah M. Anderson:

STRADDLING THE LINE
BRINGING HOME THE BACHELOR

All available now from Harlequin Desire!